THE GUNSMITH

447

Boots and Saddles

Books by J.R. Roberts
(Robert J. Randisi)

The Gunsmith series

Lady Gunsmith series

Angel Eyes series

Tracker series

Mountain Jack Pike series

COMING SOON!

The Gunsmith
448 – The Fantastic Mr. Verne

For more information visit:
www.SpeakingVolumes.us

THE GUNSMITH

447

Boots and Saddles

J.R. Roberts

SPEAKING VOLUMES, LLC
NAPLES, FLORIDA
2019

Boots and Saddles

ISBN 978-1-64540-039-4

Chapter One

Most of the men Clint Adams didn't like, over the course of his life, were a certain type. Usually, they were wealthy men—politicians, ranchers—who thought their money gave them special standing in the world. Others were cheaters and back shooters. But a man he disliked simply because of his personality was George Armstrong Custer. When Custer had his last stand at the Little Bighorn, Clint was sorry, but he didn't shed a tear. Whatever he felt was for the men who died under Custer's inept command.

He was thinking about Custer because, while seated in the lobby of the Noble House Hotel in Sacramento, he was reading about Mrs. Custer in the *Sacramento Bee* newspaper. Elizabeth Bacon Custer had written a book called *Boots and Saddles*. The paper said the book was about her life and "adventures" with her husband. The book also had a subtitle of *Life in Dakota with General Custer*.

Adventures! Custer only had adventures because he had a habit of making wrong decisions, and one of them finally got him—and his men—killed.

Clint shook his head and folded the newspaper. The Bee was covering the book because Libbie Custer was in

Sacramento promoting it. It also said she was working on a second book. He couldn't imagine she would have anything more to say about the man.

As Clint scanned the lobby, looking for Tilly Lace, the woman he was supposed to be meeting this morning, he saw three men enter, stop just inside and look around. He didn't know who they were looking for, but their eyes finally fell on him. He picked the newspaper up again.

"Mr. Adams?"

He lowered the paper. The three men were now standing in front of him. They all wore expensive suits of clothes, but they were ill-fitting on the man who stood in the center. He was short and portly, but the deference with which the other men offered him made it obvious he was in charge. It was the man to his right who had spoken.

"Mr. Adams, Mr. McMay would like to speak with you."

"And who is Mr. McMay?" Clint asked.

"I am," the man in the center said. The other men started to speak again, but McMay silenced him with a wave of his pudgy hand.

"May I speak to you?" McMay asked. "That is, if you are Clint Adams."

"I am," Clint said, "and you may, but it'll have to be right here. I'm waiting for someone."

"No problem," McMay said. "May I sit?"

Clint indicated the space beside him on the lobby divan. McMay gestured to the two men, making them cross to the other side of the lobby and sit.

"I have a proposition for you, Mr. Adams," McMay said.

"What kind of proposition?"

"Money."

"I don't hire my gun, Mr. McMay."

"That's not precisely what I'm after, although it would be part of the deal."

"And what deal is that?"

"I'm a publisher, sir," McMay said. "At present, I'm here promoting one of my authors, who is planning yet another tome."

"And what has that got to do with me?" Clint asked.

"I believe you knew the author's husband," McMay said.

"And who is your author?" Clint asked.

McMay saw the page Clint had folded the newspaper over to, and set his hand upon it.

"Elizabeth Bacon Custer," he said. "George Armstrong Custer's wife."

"Ah."

"Did you know him?"

"I did."

"Were you . . . friends?"

"Not at all," Clint said. "Truth be told, I didn't like the man."

"I see," McMay said. "And had you ever met Mrs. Custer?"

"I never had that pleasure."

"Well," McMay went on, "as I said, she's planning another book, but she needs to do some research for it. That would make it necessary for her to travel."

"Travel to where?"

"In the footsteps of her husband," the publisher said. "Although, in truth, she was with him most of the time, living on the plains during those postbellum years of reconstruction."

"I don't understand," Clint said. "What is it you want from me?"

"She needs someone to accompany her," McMay said, "someone who can keep her safe. You see, that's where your gun would come in. I mean, I'm not actually trying to hire your gun, but it is part of you."

"I see," Clint said. "You want to hire me as both guide, and protector."

"Exactly," McMay said. "I knew you'd see—"

"I'm sorry," Clint said, cutting him off, "but I'm not interested."

"You haven't heard my offer."

"The money has nothing to do with it."

"Then it's your . . . dislike for General Custer, himself?"

"That's a large part of it."

"But you have no dislike for Mrs. Custer."

"Because I've never met her."

"Well," McMay said, "maybe we can do something about that. Tomorrow night she'll be speaking to a group at a local library. Why don't you come, give a listen, and then afterward you can meet the lady."

"To what end," Clint said.

"Maybe I haven't made her needs clear," McMay said, "She can tell you herself why she needs help, and then you can make a more . . . informed decision."

Clint thought it over, came to the decision that he might as well give the woman a chance to speak for herself.

"All right," Clint said. "You can tell the lady I'll come by to listen to her."

"Excellent!" McMay stood up, smiled happily. "See you then, sir."

Chapter Two

As the three men left the hotel lobby, Chantilly Lace entered.

Clint had gone to the theater the night before to hear a reading by his friend, Mark Twain. At a party afterward, as he shared a drink with Twain, who he hadn't seen for a while, a beautiful woman came over to tell the author how much she enjoyed him.

"Allow me to present my friend, Clint Adams," Twain said, with a sparkle in his eye.

"My pleasure," she said.

"Miss Lace," Clint said.

"Please," she said, "call me Tilly."

"Not Chantilly?" he asked. "It's such a pretty name."

"Chantilly Lace?" she responded, looking askance. "What a horrible name. I don't know what my parents were thinking. No, Tilly may be an old biddy's name, but it's still better than Chantilly."

"Well," Clint said, "I don't think you ever have to worry about looking like a biddy."

"You're very sweet," she said.

She couldn't have been more than thirty years old, was wearing a blue dress that flared at the hips, hiding whether or not the rest of her body lived up to her lovely, full bosom. Her coal black hair was piled up on her head, revealing a long, pale, gracefully arched neck.

"There's a feller over there I wanna give a piece of my mind," Twain said. "Clint, you entertain this here lovely lady."

"Don't worry, Sam."

"Sam?" she asked, as Twain moved away.

"He and I are old friends, so he's Sam Clemens to me."

"Oh, I see," she said. "and are you a writer, as well, Mr. Adams?"

"Hardly," he said. "I . . . wander through life, and the only observations I make are in my head, not on paper."

"But you read?"

"I do," Clint said. "It's a way to while away the hours alone on the trail, or in my hotel room."

"Really?" she asked, the fingertips of her right hand stroked the smooth skin of her décolletage. "I would think a man like you could think of other more interesting ways to while away the time."

"A man like me?"

"I'm embarrassed," she said. "I know you're not a writer. I recognized your name."

"Ah, I see."

"Don't get me wrong," she said, "I did come here to listen to Mr. Twain read, but then I saw you with him . . . I thought I would come over and meet you both."

"So you didn't know who I was before you came over."

"Oh, no," she said, "you just looked like an interesting, handsome man standing with Mr. Twain."

"And when you're not trying to meet interesting, handsome men, what are you doing, Tilly?"

"I design dresses," she said. "In fact, this is one of mine."

She stepped back and did a quick twirl.

"Do you like it?"

"I do," he said. "It's a good color on you. It's just . . ."

She frowned.

"What? You don't like it?"

"It hides you," he said.

Now she smiled.

"Ah, but that's the point," she said. "The bodice shows promise, and the skirt conceals a secret."

"I see."

"Why?" she asked. "Are you wondering if I have a broad bottom?"

"The thought had crossed my mind," he said. "What I can see is very promising."

"Well then," she said, "perhaps we should go some-where so you can see the rest?"

Chapter Three

Her rooms were closer to the event than his hotel, so she asked if he minded going there. Considering what he thought was waiting for him, he wouldn't have minded going into an alley with her.

First, he made sure he said goodbye to Sam Clemens.

"Leavin' with the young lady?" Twain asked.

"I thought I might."

"Yeah, I thought you might, too, when I saw her," Twain said with a lecherous grin. "I'll be leavin' tomorrow. It was good seein' you again. Stop by next time you're near Hannibal."

"You know I will," Clint said, shaking the author's hand.

He walked back over to where Tilly was waiting.

"Ready?" she asked.

"I'm ready," he said. "Lead the way."

She led him out of the theater and into a cab, which took them several miles before stopping in front of a three-story building.

"I'm on the top floor," she said, taking his hand and leading him up the stairs.

When they got to the top, she handed him her keys and allowed him to unlock the door. They went inside and he gave her back her keys.

"Relax," she said. "Pour us some drinks. I'm going to get comfortable."

She went into another room, presumably her bedroom. Clint walked over to a table under a window where there were a few bottles. He would have preferred beer, but he poured two glasses of sherry, which she obviously preferred.

When she came back out moments later, she was wearing a frilly robe, belted at the waist. It was now clear that her lower half was at least as good as the upper half.

"Thank you," she said, accepting the glass of sherry. "Would you like to sit?"

"I don't think we came up here to sit," he said.

He put his drink down, took hers from her hand and set it down, then put his arms around her. She came willingly, and the kiss they shared went on for some time. He enjoyed the fullness of her body pressed up against him. He hoped she was also enjoying the parts of him that were pressed up against her.

"Yes," she said, when the kiss ended, "you're right. We didn't come up here to sit."

She took his hand and led him into the bedroom. Once there she turned, with the bed right behind her, and undid the belt of her robe. When she shrugged it off, it pooled around her ankles. She stood there, gloriously naked.

The fullness of her dark-nippled breasts took his breath away. Her hips and thighs hinted at the delights of her butt, which he would see in moments.

"Your turn," she said, waving at his clothes. "Would you like some help?"

"I've got it," he said.

He started by hanging his gunbelt on her bedpost, then removed the remainder of his clothes while she watched with a smile. When his hard, jutting cock came into view, her smile widened.

"Oh, yes," she said, closing the distance between them and taking his erection in her hot hands. She stroked it while she leaned in for another kiss.

He ran his hands down her smooth back until he reached her butt, then filled his hands, eminently satisfied with what he was holding.

The kiss went on for a long time, like the first, but they broke it because they both wanted to go further.

She smiled at him and led him the rest of the way to the bed, tugging on his long, hard cock so he had no choice but to follow.

They got onto the bed together, and then began to crawl all over each other.

Tilly's curves created peaks and valleys that Clint explored thoroughly, using his hands and his mouth. She moaned and cradled his head while he licked and bit her nipples, then kissed his way down so he could concentrate on her smooth inner thighs.

Her flesh was hot and silky, and he worked on it with his tongue until she was writhing beneath him. At that point, he switched his attention to her wet pussy. He licked the length of it, causing her to spasm as if struck by lightning. He continued to work on her with his tongue and lips, at the same time inserting first one finger, and then a second into her. She gasped and moved her hips in rhythm with his hand and mouth, and before long she was gushing all over his face, and the bed sheet.

When her spasms subsided, he mounted her and drove his hard cock deep inside her, because at that moment his satisfaction was all consuming. He slid his hands beneath her butt and held on as he drove in and out of her, causing her to gasp, grunt and cry out at different times. Then he released her butt and spread himself atop her, moved in and out of her that way so he could also concentrate on her nipples and her mouth . . .

***

Later in the night, she woke him with her mouth. She was kissing his neck, then his shoulders. As he woke, she moved to his nipples and emulated what he had done earlier, and kissed her way down his body to his thighs. But instead of licking him there, she immediately went to his thickening cock, first running her tongue up and down it until it glistened with her saliva, and was hard as a rock. Then she opened her hot mouth and took him inside.

As she sucked him avidly, he held her head in his hands, and moved his hips to match the bobbing motion of her head. She released him every so often so she could pump his penis with one hand, while fondling his balls with the other. Then she'd take it back into her mouth again. Finally, as he felt his release rumble up through his legs and thighs, he took hold of the bedrail above his head, opened his mouth and roared out loud as he exploded into her mouth . . .

***

He woke the next morning with her lying on his left arm, his right arm still free to grab his gun, if the need arose. Her sweet flesh was pressed against the length of him. She was sleeping soundly, and he was able to slip out from beneath her without waking her. He dressed, and left a note asking her to meet him in the lobby of his hotel that night for supper. And then he left her rooms, and went back to his own.

Chapter Four

So he remained in the lobby, after the publisher, McMay, left, and waited for Miss Chantilly Lace to come. It took half-an-hour, but she finally appeared and approached him in a swirl of blue skirts.

"Where are we going?" she asked.

He stood.

"To Delmonico's," he said. "For the best steak Sacramento."

"And after?" she asked.

"I don't know," he said. "Why don't we talk about that after?"

As they walked through the lobby, she asked, "How long do you plan on staying in Sacramento?"

"I've already been here longer than I planned," he said. "So the answer is, I don't know."

"Well, good," she said, linking her arm in his left one. "Then I don't have to worry you'll disappear at a moment's notice."

"No," he assured her, "not at a moment's notice."

***

They talked over excellent steaks, about her business, her childhood, two failed marriages, and then she sat back and fell silent.

"What is it?" he asked.

"You," she said. "You haven't told me anything about you."

"You know about me," he said. "You know who I am, and what my reputation is."

"But do I know the real you?"

"After last night?" he asked, "More than most people."

"But we didn't talk."

"We didn't have to, if I remember correctly."

He reached for her hand, but she pulled it back.

"No, no," she said, "this time I want to talk."

"About what?"

"About you," she said. "About who you are, what you are, where you came from. . ."

"I'm afraid not," he said.

"But why?"

"My past is my past," he said. "I don't discuss it."

"Come on," she said, "I bet I can find some newspaper interviews."

"No," he said, "you can't, because I don't allow interviews."

"By anybody?"

"By anybody," he said.

She frowned.

"Dessert?" he asked.

"Yes," she said, "an expensive one."

***

After she destroyed a chocolate mousse, they left the restaurant and were able to walk back to his hotel.

"Your place, this time?" she asked, in the lobby.

"It's closer," he said.

"That suits me."

They walked up to the second floor to his room, where he unlocked the door, opened it, stuck his head in, and then allowed her to enter first.

"Do you always have to do that?" she asked.

"Do what?"

"Check first to see if anyone's in your room."

"Pretty much," he said. "It's one of the reasons I'm still alive."

"Oh, my," she said. "That must be a horrible way to have to live."

"Live," he said, "is the operative word, here."

Chapter Five

Tilly rose first in the morning, explaining that she had things to attend to in the morning.

"What about tonight?" he asked.

"What did you have in mind?" she asked, while he watched her dress.

"I'm going to a library," he said.

"A what?"

"A library."

"Why would you do that?"

"I'm going to listen to Mrs. George Armstrong Custer talk about a book she wrote about her husband."

She stopped and looked at him. "Custer?"

"That's right."

"You mean the Custer's Last Stand, that Custer?" she asked. "The Little Bighorn and all that?"

"Exactly."

She shivered and said, "How gruesome." Fully dressed, she faced him. "I think I'll pass. Besides, I have something else to do tonight."

"All right, then," he said. "I don't know what I'll be doing after tonight."

"I know where you are," Tilly said. She came to the bed and kissed him, then left.

J.R. Roberts

***

Clint spent the rest of the day in his hotel, first having breakfast in the diningroom, then going back to his room to read some Twain. Libbie Custer's appearance at the library was going to be before dinner, so on the off chance that he would end up dining with her, he wore his best suit of clothes, the one he had been wearing when he met Tilly at the theater.

He went out the front door and told the doorman he needed a cab.

"Where to, sir?"

"The Mansfield Library."

"Yes, sir."

The doorman got him a cab drawn by a single horse, held the door open while he stepped into the open air rear seat.

"The gentleman is going to the Mansfield Library," the doorman said.

"Yessir," the driver snapped.

He got the horse going and in twenty minutes pulled up in front of the library. Unlike other drivers Clint had over the years, this one had not tried to have a conversation over his shoulder.

"You want me to wait?" the driver asked, as Clint stepped down.

"No, that's all right," Clint said, paying him, "I'll find my way back."

"Suit yerself," the driver said, and drove off.

As he entered the lobby of the library, he saw well-dressed people standing around with drinks in their hands. One of them was the publisher, McMay. He realized he had no idea what the man's first name was.

McMay saw him and waved him over. The two men who had accompanied him to the hotel were standing on either side of him.

"Randall," he said to one of them, "get the man a glass of champagne."

Randall moved off very quickly, so Clint had no chance to say he didn't want one.

"Where is Mrs. Custer?" he asked.

"They gave her a special room to prepare in," McMay said. "She's very excited that you agreed to come."

"I'm looking forward to meeting her."

"It'll have to be after her talk," McMay said.

"That's fine," Clint said. "I'm here to listen to her, like everyone else."

"That's good," McMay said. "Here's your champagne."

"Thank you, Randall," Clint said.

Randall, a man in his early thirties, looked surprised at having been addressed.

"Um, you're welcome."

Clint sipped as little of his drink as possible.

"Who are all these people?" he asked. "Professionals, like you?"

"They better not be," McMay said. "I'm her one and only publisher. She doesn't need another. No, these people are all here to listen to her speak, and hopefully buy her book. Which we'll be selling in the lobby afterward."

"I see."

"And Libbie will be out here, talking to people and signing books," McMay explained. "But first we'll take you back to meet her. We won't be asking you to come out here and buy one of her books."

"That suits me," Clint said.

"Very well, then," McMay said. "We better go and get to our seats. Mr. Adams, will you sit with us?"

"Definitely," Clint said. "Just lead the way."

Chapter Six

McMay led Clint into an auditorium that had a full stage in front of it. They went right down to the first row and sat down. On the stage was a chair, and a table with a glass of water on it. Clint had seen Twain and Buffalo Bill Cody do it, but no one else.

"Is anyone going to introduce her or will she just walk out?" Clint asked.

"The head librarian will introduce her, as soon as the seats fill."

Clint turned and looked at the people who were drifting in. Even if all of the folks who had been in the lobby came in, he thought McMay was being pretty optimistic about the seats filling.

"There he is now." McMay turned to look at the room, and his face fell. "I had hoped for better attendance." He turned back to the stage. His two yes-men were on his right, and they both looked worried.

"Ladies and gentlemen," the man on stage said, "we are very pleased to have with us tonight at our library, Mrs. Elizabeth Bacon Custer, who will be discussing the book she's written about her husband, George Armstrong Custer. Please welcome Mrs. Custer."

There was some scattered applause as Libbie Custer came onto the stage.

Libbie Custer surprised Clint. He knew she had to be in her forties. But she looked ten years younger than that—and lovely. She was dressed in a tight-fitting dress that hugged her bosom and waist, and then flared.

She said thank you to the assemblage, then sat down in the chair they had supplied for her and started talking about her husband. It was obvious by the language, and her verve for her subject, that she considered her husband to be a hero. While she spoke, some people in the audience became antsy, and eventually some men began to heckle her.

"You gotta be kiddin'," one yelled.

"We all know your husband woulda been court-martialed if he had lived," another shouted.

"My husband was a brave man who found himself in an untenable position," she said, calmly.

"That's a load of bull crap!" someone else shouted. "He got all those men killed because he didn't know what he was doin'. Just because you wrote a book about him don't change that."

Now others began to shout.

The head of the library came out onto the stage and tried to calm things down. He put one hand on Libbie's shoulder with the other waved at the audience.

"Please!" he called. "Please! This is not what we're here for."

"Yeah," some shouted back, "and we ain't here to be lied to, either."

"I don't understand what lies you think this woman has told you."

"Well," someone else shouted, "why don't we start with her saying her husband was brave, and a hero."

Libbie Custer surprised everyone by jumping to her feet.

"Would you believe somebody else?" she asked. "Would you believe he was a brave hero if you heard it from someone other than his wife?"

That brought laughter from the heckling group, which Clint could now see was right in the center. They had obviously come here for this purpose.

Libbie Custer raised her voice.

"Would the Gunsmith do?"

Everyone stopped and it got quiet.

"This is not a good idea," Clint said.

"Why not?" McMay asked.

"Because I don't think George Custer was a hero."

"Maybe you could lie?"

"I'll try."

"You sayin' the Gunsmith is here?" a man shouted. "Listenin' to you?"

"Yes," she said, "and he was my husband's friend. So he can tell you I'm not lying."

"Nononono," Clint said, in a whisper.

"What's wrong?" McMay asked. "You knew him, right?"

"Yes, but we were never friends."

"Like I said," McMay said. "This situation may call for a little lying if we don't want this crowd to pull us apart."

"Crowd?"

McMay sighed.

"I guess you're right," he admitted. "It's better that more people didn't show up."

"Mr. Adams is right here in the first row," Libbie said. "Clint, will you stand up and talk to these people about my husband?"

As Clint started to stand McMay said, "You either have to lie, or shoot all these people."

"Shooting them might be easier," Clint told him, and turned to face the audience.

Chapter Seven

"George Armstrong Custer," Clint said, slowly because he was still trying to come up with something to say, "was a soldier."

Everybody waited for more.

Except for one man.

"How do we know you're the Gunsmith?" The man stood up and said. He happened to be wearing a bowler hat. It was a big enough target.

Clint drew and shot the hat from his head.

"Does anybody need more proof than that?" Libbie Custer asked.

The man sat down and Clint holstered his gun. He would have to replace the round later.

"As I was saying," he continued, "Custer was a soldier, and he was an officer, and you can't say that about men unless they have courage."

"He was a hero, wasn't he, Mr. Adams?" Libbie called from stage.

Clint thought quickly and then said, "He was . . . heroic. There was no doubt about that. And now I think you should all let this woman continue with what she was saying . . . or get up and leave."

He didn't know if they stayed to hear what else Libbie Custer had to say, or because they were afraid he would shoot something off them if they got up to leave.

Clint turned, waved his arm at Libbie, said "Continue, Mrs. Custer," and sat down.

McMay patted him on the arm and said, "Well done."

***

Afterward Libbie Custer walked off stage to a smattering of applause, and then people apparently felt it was safe enough for them to leave.

"Okay," McMay said, "let's get back there. I think she's going to need us."

Clint followed McMay and his yes-men backstage to the room the library had given Libbie.

McMay knocked on the door and entered, even though Clint hadn't heard a word from inside.

Libbie Custer was sitting in the center of the room in a wooden chair, her hands in her lap. That was all the library had given her, a chair.

"That was awful," she said.

"It was bad," McMay agreed, "but it wasn't your fault."

"No," she said, "it wasn't. It was yours," she pointed at him, "and yours," she pointed at Clint.

"Mine?" Clint asked. "What did I do?"

"You hedged."

"He did what?" McMay asked.

"He hedged," she said, again. "He was supposed to talk about what a hero my husband was. Instead he said that stuff about a soldier and an officer having to be brave, and that George was heroic. Not a hero, just heroic."

"Mrs. Custer," Clint said, "I met your husband several times. I didn't know him well, and we weren't friends— as you told that audience—and to tell you the honest truth, I don't think he was a good officer, or a hero."

"What?" she squawked. "What?"

"Now Libbie—" McMay started.

"This is the man in whose hands you want to put me?" she demanded of McMay.

"I'd still like to know how what happened out there was also Mr. McMay's fault."

Libbie Custer glared at Clint.

"He was in charge of getting people here," she said. "It was supposed to be people who wanted to hear what I had to say."

"Actually," McMay said, and pointed at his man, Randall, "that was his job."

"You're going to blame your employee?" she demanded.

"You're blaming us," Clint reminded her. "Maybe you just didn't make your point convincingly."

She jumped to her feet and faced him.

"My point is and always will be that my husband was a great man!"

"You'll find a lot of people familiar with the Little Bighorn who would disagree with that."

She turned to McMay, ignoring Clint.

"I'd like to go to my hotel," she said. "I don't suppose we have any people waiting out there to buy a book."

"No, I suppose not," McMay said.

"And I don't want this man to accompany us!" She pointed at Clint.

"That suits me," Clint said.

He had not intended to accompany them to her hotel, but he did walk out to the lobby with them, where they were all surprised. There were actually people waiting in line, holding a copy of her book to be signed.

"Libbie . . ." McMay said.

"Oh yes, very well!"

Chapter Eight

Clint flagged down a cab out in front of the library, was about to get in when Randall came running out of the library.

"Mr. Adams."

Clint stopped and turned to face the man.

"Yes?"

"Mr. McMay wonders if you would wait and speak with him before you leave? Please?"

Clint was sure the please was coming from Randall, and not McMay.

"Does he pay you well for what you do?" Clint asked.

Randall looked surprised by the question.

"Uh, no, sir."

"Then why do you do it?"

"I want to be in publishing."

Clint nodded.

"Does he want to talk inside?"

"No," Randall said, "he asked that I take you to a small saloon around the corner."

"And who's taking Mrs. Custer back to her hotel?" Clint asked.

"That would be Cedric," Randall said. "He, my, uh, the other one that Mr. McMay doesn't really pay well."

The other yes-man.

"All right, Randall," Clint said. "Let's go and get a drink. Lead on."

***

The place was right around the corner from the library, as Randall had said. In fact, even though it was not connected to the larger building, it had a sign on it that read LIBRARY SALOON.

Inside it seemed half-filled with businessmen from the surrounding buildings. Clint was sure he was in the midst of lawyers and judges and financial wizards.

"There," he said to Randall, "in the back."

"Mr. McMay won't see us."

"But we'll see him. Don't worry."

They walked to the table and sat, a pretty young girl dressed much more sedately than most saloon girls Clint had seen, came over.

"Evening, gents. What can I get you?"

"Champagne?" Randall asked Clint.

"Hell, no," Clint said. "Beer."

"Two beers, please," Randall said to the girl.

"Comin' right up." Clint detected an Irish lilt to her tone.

She brought the beers and told them to let her know when they needed something else.

"Mr. Randall," Clint said, "to your health."

"Thank you, sir."

They raised their glasses.

"Well, that was a huge farce, wasn't it?" Clint said.

"Yes, sir, it was. Did you really not like General Custer?"

"I loathed him," Clint said.

"Why, sir?"

"Call me Clint, not sir," Clint said.

"Yes, sir, uh, Clint."

"And is Randall your first name?

"Last," Randall said. "Mr. McMay calls us all by our last names. I'm Lucius."

"Well, Lucius, you asked me why I loathed George Armstrong Custer. It's because he was a conceited blowhard, a dunderhead, and a dandy who danced his way to his position. And when the time came for him to make a real contribution, he got all his men killed at the Little Bighorn."

"Jesus," Randall said, "so he really wasn't a hero?"

"Not in the least."

"But she—"

"She's his wife," Clint said. "What else is she going to think, or say?"

"But . . . she's writing books about him."

"Again," Clint said, "what else is she going to do?"

"I guess that'll depend on how fast Mr. McMay can talk," Randall said.

At that point the publisher entered and looked around for them. Randall started to stand.

"No, Lucius," Clint said, putting his hand out, "let him find us on his own."

It took a few minutes, but the publisher finally saw them and walked over.

"I'm glad you decided to stay and talk," McMay said to Clint.

"Thank young Lucius," Clint said, slapping the man on the back. "He was very convincing."

"Lucius?"

"Lucius Randall," Clint said.

"Oh," McMay said, "yes, of course. What are you two drinking?"

"Beer," Clint said. "I prefer it to champagne."

The waitress came over and McMay managed to get out the one word, "Beer," and sat down.

Chapter Nine

"I asked you to lie," McMay said, when he had his beer.

"I did," Clint said.

"You said Custer was a hero."

"Even his wife didn't hear me say that."

"So she was right. You—what did she call it—hedged?"

"I did. As I told Lucius, here, Custer was no friend of mine. He was an idiot, and a dandy."

"Then how did he get a woman like that to be loyal to him, even in death?" Lucius asked.

McMay looked at him, as if surprised he had spoken.

"What can I say?" Clint asked. "She loved him."

Lucius shook his head and said, "Women."

"I know!" Clint said. Then he looked at McMay. "What did you want to talk to me about?"

"The same thing as before."

"Oh, you mean to tell me Libbie Custer still wants my help?" Clint asked. "If she ever wanted it at all."

"That was a slight exaggeration," McMay said. "Although when I mentioned your name she did agree."

"Because she thought I was her husband's friend?"

"She said she had heard you mentioned by him with respect," the publisher said.

"You're kidding."

"Respect," McMay added, "and dislike."

"Well, we shared the second one," Clint said, "but not the first."

"Why can't you just fake it?" McMay asked.

"Look," Clint said, "I've known a lot of men who died while doing their absolute best. I can't abide a man who died doing his worst, and took all his men with him."

"All right," McMay said, "you didn't like the man. What about his wife?"

"Well, I just met her today, but it seems we have a healthy dislike for each other."

"Nonsense," McMay said. "She was just . . . upset."

"Yes, she was."

"Mr. Adams—may I call you Clint?"

"I don't even know your first name," Clint pointed out. "Let's keep it at Mr. Adams, for now."

"As you wish . . . Mr. Adams, Mrs. Custer needs you desperately."

"She needs someone, you mean."

"No," McMay insisted, "she needs you. You saw what happened out there. If you hadn't been there, they would've torn her to pieces."

"Isn't that a little dramatic?" Clint asked.

"I don't mean literally," McMay said. "They wouldn't have stopped when they did. For all we know, they brought rotted fruit to throw at her."

Clint frowned.

"This is a research trip?"

"Yes," McMay said, "but she'll also be promoting where and when she can."

"Where, specifically?"

"Where she says she was stationed with her husband in his early days in the army," McMay said. "Texas and Kansas."

"Those people don't forget things like the Little Bighorn, Mr. McMay," Clint pointed out.

"Exactly why she needs you!" McMay snapped.

"You think after today she still wants me?" Clint asked.

"We can talk to her," McMay said, "you and I. Make her understand the dangers. I can't have this woman go out there and get killed."

Clint still thought McMay was being dramatic, but then on the Great Plains anything could happen. There were probably still Indians out there who remembered Custer.

"What do you say?" McMay asked.

"I say have another beer," Clint replied, "and tell me your first name."

***

They each had another beer while Clint thought the situation over. If he allowed Libbie Custer to go to the Plains alone, and he heard that something had happened to her, how would he feel about it?

Well, he'd feel bad for her, of course, but would he feel guilty knowing he'd had the opportunity to possibly keep her safe?

"What do you have to say, Mr. Adams?" McMay asked.

"I'm considering it."

"Shall I tell you how much I'm willing to pay you?" the publisher asked.

"I assumed you'd cover the expense of the entire trip," Clint said.

"That's correct."

"Then you'll do it?" McMay asked.

"I think," Clint said, "we should put the question to the lady and allow her to make the final decision."

Chapter Ten

Clint went to their hotel, The Federal, with McMay—who finally admitted his first name was Henry—and Lucius Randall. It was also where Libbie Custer was staying, in a large suite of rooms.

They entered the lobby and McMay held up his hands and stopped.

"I'd better go up and talk to her first," McMay said, "see if she has calmed down."

"Hey," Clint said, "if she won't see me, that'll be the answer."

"Don't worry," McMay said, "she'll at least do that."

Clint slapped Randall on the shoulder and said, "Me and Lucius will go to the bar and have another drink."

"Fine," said McMay, "I'll look for you there."

As he continued across the lobby, Clint grabbed Randall's arm and propelled him toward the doorway that led to the bar.

When they each had a beer in their hand Randall said, "You're confusing him."

"How so?"

"You're treating me like I'm a person."

"That's how he should be treating you."

"Oh, to him Cedric and I are just like . . . office furniture."

"Well, out here a man should be treated like a man," Clint said. "Maybe you ought to tell him that."

"He would fire me for sure," Randall said. "I just have to wait until he's ready to move me to another job in his company."

"Why not go to another company?" Clint asked.

Randall rolled his eyes.

"Then I'd have to start all over again, from the bottom," Randall said. "No, no, I've put too much time into this already. Don't worry about me, Mr. Adams, I know what I'm doing."

"Well," Clint said, "as long as you do, I guess I should butt out."

Randall changed the subject.

"Do you think she'll see you after what happened?"

"I guess that's going to depend on how convincing your boss is."

"He can be pretty persuasive when he wants to be," Randall admitted.

"We should know soon."

It was another ten minutes before McMay came back down.

"All right," he said, taking a seat, "she'll see you, but she wants to do it alone, just the two of you."

"In her room?" Clint asked.

"Yes," McMay said.

"And how do you feel about that?"

"You just go," the publisher said, "Randall and I will wait here." He looked at the younger man. "He can tell me what you and he have been talking about."

"All right, then," Clint said, standing. "Just tell me her room number."

***

Clint left the bar, walked across the lobby to the stairway, went up to the second floor and down the hall to the door of Libbie Custer's suite. He was completely open to how this meeting would go, but he hoped better than their first.

When she opened the door to his knock, he saw she had changed into a bathrobe, tightly belted at the waist. Her hair was still up, the way she had worn it for her event.

"If you believe for one moment that I'm going to sleep with you," she said, "you are mistaken!"

He just stared at her, stunned.

"As long as you can deal with that, you might as well come in," she said, backing away.

He entered and closed the door behind him.

"What the hell are you talking about?" he demanded.

"I know your reputation, Mr. Adams," she said, "with a gun and with the ladies. In fact, George told me you thought every woman in the world should sleep with you."

"Then is it any wonder we didn't like each other?" Clint asked.

"Perhaps not."

She stood in the center of the room with her arms folded.

"All right," she said, "perhaps I've been unfair. You didn't have to like George. I'm aware that not many men did. He was . . . intimidating."

That wasn't the word Clint was going to supply, but he let it go.

"I suppose we should deal with the matter at hand." She turned to face him. "Will you help me?"

"Your publisher has had a lot to say," Clint said, "but I'd like to hear why you think you need help."

"I'll be a woman travelling alone," she said. "Please, sit."

She sat down on the sofa, and he sat in a matching chair. The suite offered her a very large sitting room, with an adjoining bedroom next to it, which he could see through the door.

"My husband's detractors . . . even enemies . . . will not be kind, Mr. Adams," she said. "You heard all those people today, and they didn't even know him."

"And why are you making this trip?" Clint asked.

"I'm doing it to collect material for a second book," she said. "My publisher, Henry, is happy with this one, and wants me to do another."

"And do you want to write another book?"

"Of course!" she said. "I like nothing better than writing about my husband."

Well, apparently people liked reading about him, too, which Clint didn't understand.

Chapter Eleven

As Clint re-entered the bar, he saw Randall drinking beer while McMay once again was working on a glass of champagne. When he saw Clint he came half out of his chair.

"What happened?" he asked. "You just went up."

"We agreed that I didn't like her husband—"

"—damn it, Adams—"

"—and she asked me to go with her."

"She did?" Randall asked.

McMay sat back down.

"What did you say?"

Clint sat. His previous beer was still there, but had gone warm, so he left it.

"I agreed to travel with her."

"That's wonderful!" McMay said.

"She told me you're making all her arrangements," Clint said.

"Well," McMay said, "anything that can be done by stage coach or train."

"That's okay," Clint said. "I'll take care of everything else." He leaned forward and looked at McMay. "If I'm going to do this, it all has to be left in my hands once she and I get going."

"Understood."

"I'll ask for your assistance when I need it."

"And you'll get it."

"And I want Lucius, here, to come with us."

McMay and Randall both said, "What?"

"I'll need an extra pair of hands for . . . incidentals," Clint said.

Both men remained silent.

"What do you say, Lucius?" Clint asked.

"Wait—" McMay started, but Clint cut him off.

"There's nothing for you to say, Mr. McMay, unless Randall agrees to go."

Clint and McMay looked at Lucius Randall.

"Can you ride?" Clint asked.

"Well, sure."

"And shoot?"

"I can shoot," Randall said, "whether or not I can hit anything—"

"That's not important," Clint said. "Do you want to come?"

"Well . . . sure, okay."

Clint looked at McMay.

"You're footing the bills," Clint said. "Okay if he comes?"

"What does Libbie say?"

"She says she likes him," Clint said. "She wouldn't mind if he came along."

McMay looked at Randall.

"All right," the publisher said. "I'll make travel arrangements for three. Where to first?"

"Austin, Texas," Clint said.

"When?"

"Today's Tuesday," Clint said. "Make it Thursday morning. I've got some things to do." He looked at Randall. "Can you be ready by then?"

"Yes, sir."

"Good," Clint said. "Then let's have another drink on it."

"I have to make plans," McMay said, "so I'll say good-night."

"I'll come along, sir—" Randall said, preparing to stand.

"No, no," McMay said, "you and Clint stay and have another drink. I'll pay the tab on the way out. I'll come by your hotel in the afternoon, Mr. Adams, with all the details."

"Good," Clint said. "I'll see you then."

McMay stopped at the bar, paid the bill, and left. Clint waved to the bartender for two more beers, the man nodded and brought them over. There were no girls working in the hotel bar at the moment.

"Why'd you do that?" Randall asked.

"I'll need somebody else along," Clint said. "I only thought of you at the last minute, thought I'd give you an opportunity. You took it."

"Yeah, I did," Randall said. "I can't believe it, but I did."

They drank.

"Did Mrs. Custer really say that?" he asked. "That she liked me?"

"She said she didn't care who came as long as it wasn't Cedric," Clint said.

"Yeah," Randall said, "Cedric can be . . . well, Cedric."

"Do you have a horse?" Clint asked.

"No," Randall said, "we all came here by train."

"All right, in the morning we—that is, Mr. McMay— will buy you one."

"Will you help me pick it out?"

"I will," Clint said. "Don't worry. In fact, why don't we wait until we get to Austin, and then we can buy a horse for you and Mrs. Custer."

"What about you?"

"I have my horse with me," Clint said. "We'll put him in the stock car of the train."

"Should I buy a gun?" Randall asked. "I mean, you asked me if I can shoot."

"You don't have a gun?"

"You don't really need one in publishing."

"What are you more comfortable with?" Clint asked. "A handgun or a rifle?"

"I'm more experienced with a rifle," Randall said. "I mean, just for hunting."

"Okay, we'll take care of that, too, when we get to Austin."

"And what's in Austin?" Randall asked. "I mean, why are we going there?"

"It's a jumping off point," Clint said. "We'll be heading to Hempstead."

"What's there?"

"It was an early posting for Custer, and Libbie was with him. She wants to have a look at it now."

They finished the beers and stood to leave.

"I'm going to wait to hear from McMay at my hotel tomorrow," Clint said, as they went to the lobby. "I assume I'll see you when I see him."

"I'm sure that's how it will go." The two men shook hands. "Thank you so much for this, Mr. Adams."

"If you're going to be riding with me," Clint said, "you're going to have to call me Clint."

"I'll do that, Clint."

The younger man crossed the lobby to the stairs that led to the second floor, while Clint turned and went out the front door.

Chapter Twelve

Clint spent the night in his room alone, ate breakfast the same way the next morning, then went to the livery to check on Eclipse.

"Looks like we'll be back on the trail soon, boy," he said, slapping the Darley's thick neck.

"He's ready, Mr. Adams," the hostler told him. "I been takin' good care of him."

"I can see that," Clint said. "Thanks."

He left the livery with the intention of heading back to his hotel. Instead, he found four men waiting outside the stable for him. They stood in a semi-circle, with the stable behind him.

"Hello, boys," Clint said. "What's on your mind?"

"You and Custer," one of them said. Clint immediately recognized his voice—and bowler—from the library the night before.

"No, no, don't tell me, let me guess," Clint said, pointing to each of them. "You're the idiots who were heckling Mrs. Custer last night."

"We're the idiots who are gonna teach you a lesson," the man said.

The speaker was the man whose hat he had shot off. Clint dropped his hand down to his gun, but didn't draw it. He didn't think he would need to.

"We ain't armed, Mr. Gunsmith," the spokesman said. "If you shoot down four unarmed citizens, you're gonna be in a lot of trouble."

"So you think I should just keep my gun holstered and let the four of you pummel me?"

One of the other men pointed to the spokesman and said, "He told us you would."

"Well, he's wrong," Clint said. "There's no way I'm going to take a beating just to prove a point. No, I'd rather shoot each of you in the leg and then explain it later to the law." He put his hand on his gun. "So who's first? You?" he spoke to the man who had pointed to the spokesman.

"Hell, not me," the man said.

"Then it must be you, bowler," Clint said, pointing at the big mouth.

"You wouldn't dare," the man said.

"I shot your hat off last night," Clint said. "How about a toe, this time?"

"Lane, you fool," one of the others said, turning to leave with a dismissive wave of his hand. "Or maybe we're even bigger damn fools for followin' you here."

Another man turned, walked off, and then a third, leaving Lane there, alone, still wearing the bowler hat that had a hole in it.

"What do you say, Lane?" Clint asked. "Are you going to play the fool all alone?"

"There'll be another day, Gunsmith," Lane said.

"I don't think so," Clint said. "At least, I hope not, for your sake."

Lane turned and hurried after his friends.

"You shoulda just shot 'em."

Clint turned, saw the hostler watching the action while slumped in the doorway.

"It would have been a waste of bullets," Clint said. "Besides, you just want me to go to jail so you can keep my horse."

"What? That's not—I never—" the man stammered, standing up straight.

"Relax," Clint said. "I was kidding. Just have my horse ready to go Thursday morning."

"Yes, sir," the man promised. "I sure will."

Chapter Thirteen

Clint assumed that Libbie Custer and Lucius Randall would need at least a day to get themselves packed and ready for a trip to Austin, Texas. He himself could have been ready the next day.

That next morning, he went downstairs for breakfast and found the publisher, Henry McMay, waiting for him in the lobby.

"Do you mind if I buy you breakfast?" the man asked.

"Not at all. Is here, okay?"

"That's fine."

Clint felt there was something on McMay's mind other than where to eat breakfast.

They went into the diningroom to the table Clint had been using whenever he ate there.

"The usual, Mr. Adams?" the waiter asked.

"Yes, for both of us, please," Clint said. He looked at McMay. "Do you mind?"

"No, no, anything is fine," McMay said.

The waiter left and came back quickly with a pot of strong coffee and two cups. He poured, and promised to return laden with food.

"What's on your mind, Mr. McMay?" Clint asked. "It sure isn't food."

"I've made your travel arrangements," he said. "The three of you will be on a train tomorrow morning."

"I have to get my horse—"

"Your horse has been taken care of," McMay said. "There's a space in the stock car for it. You'll have to get it there."

"I'll get *him* there," Clint said.

"I must ask why you decided to take Randall with you?" McMay said.

"He seems to be a smart young man, and I thought I could use the extra pair of hands."

"You're going to have to be careful with him," McMay said.

"Why's that?"

"He's valuable."

"You don't treat him like he's valuable," Clint said. "He's one of your yes-men."

"For now," McMay said. "He's valuable to the future of my company."

"Then why don't you treat him that way?" Clint asked.

"Never mind," McMay said. "The way I train my employees is not your concern. I just need you to be sure you bring him back in one piece."

"Why would he not come back in one piece?" Clint asked.

"You're taking him west," McMay said. "He's not built for the West. You're going to have to look after him."

"I'll be looking after Libbie Custer," Clint pointed out, "and Lucius will be helping me do that."

"Adams . . ."

McMay trailed off, but Clint felt the man was going to come back on his own, so he waited.

"All right, look," McMay said. "I had a partner a long time ago. The company belonged to the both of us. Then . . . he died. But we were more than just partners, we were like brothers."

"I'm sorry you lost him."

"Not the point," McMay went on, gruffly. "He had a son and I promised to look after him, not let anything happen to him."

"Oh, okay," Clint said. "Lucius is the son?"

"He is," McMay said. "Now, I could try and stop him from going with you, but I doubt I'd succeed. You may not see it, but the boy has a mind of his own."

"He's hardly a boy," Clint said. "While he's with me, I'll be treating him like a man."

"Tread softly, please," McMay said.

"Give the young man some credit, McMay," Clint said, as the waiter brought out their steak-and-eggs on huge plates.

"Do you always eat like this?" McMay asked, staring at the food.

"Pretty much," Clint said, "when I'm in town. On the trail it'll be a lot lighter, mostly bacon and beans, beef jerky, maybe some biscuits."

"Well, good," McMay said, picking up his utensils, "at least Randall won't come back fat."

"Don't worry about him so much, McMay," Clint said. "We're not going anyplace where he might get hurt." Clint waited a couple of beats. "Unless there's something else you're not telling me?"

"About what?" McMay asked, sawing into his steak with great concentration.

"About Libbie Custer and what she's doing."

"She's researching another book about her life with her husband."

"And is there anyone out there who doesn't want her to do that?"

"Not anyone that I know of," McMay said.

"That was a very carefully worded response, Mr. McMay," Clint said. "I think maybe you better let me have the rest of it."

McMay chewed his first bite and said, "Very well."

Chapter Fourteen

"Libbie has received some letters."

"What kind of letters?"

"Threatening letters."

"From who?"

"She doesn't know," McMay said. "They're unsigned."

"And what do they say?"

"She'll join her husband soon, that sort of thing. Certainly nothing veiled."

"And you think whoever's threatening her will move against her during this trip?"

"That's something I'm afraid of, yes," McMay said. "But I'm sure you wouldn't let that happen, would you?"

"Naturally," Clint said. "You wouldn't want anything to happen to your cash cow."

"I am more concerned with her as a person," McMay said. "Although you may find that hard to believe."

"I'll do my best," Clint said, "to believe you, and to protect her."

"And," McMay went on, "you'd never let your feelings for her husband cause you to treat her any other way."

"There's no reason she ever has to pay for the sins of her husband," Clint said. "Not to me, anyway."

"Good to know."

"In fact," Clint said, "I'm kind of insulted you'd even mention it."

"I'm sorry," McMay said, seeing the anger in Clint's eyes. "I didn't mean . . . is there some way I can make up for it?"

"Yes," Clint said, "let's discuss my fee."

"I thought money didn't enter into this for you," McMay said.

"That was before . . ."

***

After making McMay pay for insulting him, they went on to finish their breakfast.

In the lobby once again, Clint said, "When we get to Austin, I'll need to buy outfits for both Libbie Custer and Randall—that means horses, saddles, everything."

"I'll see that you have enough cash for the task," McMay said.

"And I'll need a letter of credit," Clint added. "In case I have to go to a bank and get more of your money."

"A letter of credit?" McMay frowned. "For how much?"

"Just leave the amount blank," Clint said, and headed off across the lobby.

***

Supper that night was shared by the four of them—Clint, McMay, Randall, and Libbie Custer—at a restaurant someone had oddly named The Peppermint Steakhouse.

"How did you find this place?" Clint asked McMay.

"How could one not find a place with a name like this?" McMay responded.

"Do you know how it got its name?" Clint asked.

"According to my source, the man who owns it is named Peppermint."

"How odd," Libbie Custer said, looking around, "but it does seem to be a very popular place."

"A fitting place, I thought," McMay said, "for our farewell supper."

"Where's Cedric?" Randall wondered out loud.

"Don't worry about him," McMay said.

A waiter came over to their table and told them what was on the menu. There were two specials of the evening, one steak, and one fish. Clint and Libbie both chose the steak, while McMay and Randall went with the fish.

"What time will we be leaving tomorrow?" Libbie asked.

"Early," McMay said. "Your train leaves at eight a.m."

"Good," she said, "the sooner the better."

"Randall and I will come and fetch you at six," Clint said. "We'll have a small breakfast, then proceed to the railroad station."

"I see," she said. "So young Mr. Randall will be coming along?"

"Yes," Clint said. "I thought we could use the extra pair of hands. How many suitcases do you have?"

"Two bags, one trunk."

"A trunk?" Clint asked. "Is it necessary?"

"Yes."

"I think we can take it as far as Austin, but once there you'll have to whittle it down to one suitcase."

"How can I do that?"

"When you and your husband were assigned to a new post, did you arrive with suitcases and a trunk?"

"Trunks," she said, "many trunks."

"We're going to be on the trail, Libbie," Clint explained, "a trunk is a hinderance—a big one."

"But—"

"Give it some thought," Clint said, as the waiter came with their plates and started setting them down. "You have until Austin to figure it out."

Chapter Fifteen

Clint wasn't staying in the same hotel as McMay, Randall and Libbie Custer, so he rose even earlier that morning so he could check out and make his way over to their hotel. He found Randall and McMay waiting in the lobby for him.

"Where's Libbie?" Clint asked.

"She hasn't come down, yet," McMay said. "We might as well go into the dining room and wait."

"What about her luggage?" Clint asked.

"I had Randall and Cedric bring it down earlier," McMay said. "You can fight with her about it in Austin."

They went into the dining room and got a table. Clint was determined to eat light, as there would always be time on the train to eat if they got hungry, later.

They ordered coffee and waited to order their food until Libbie arrived, which she did fifteen minutes and a second pot of coffee later.

"I'm starved!" she said, as she sat.

"Order light," Clint said. "You're late, so we don't have much time."

"Are you going to be a harsh taskmaster this trip when it comes to time, Clint?" she asked.

"You better believe it."

***

They just managed to make their train, because Libbie had forgotten something in her room and had to run up and get it. But they were finally ensconced in their seats, with Eclipse in the stock car.

"We don't have a sleeping car?" Libbie asked.

"Sacramento to Austin is not that bad," Clint said. "We'll be fine in the passenger car."

"And where are my bags?" she asked. "I hope they're not still on the platform."

"Your bags were loaded onto the train, Mrs. Custer," Randall said. "I assure you."

"Thank you, Lucius," she said. "It's nice to see that someone is concerned about my bags."

"I'm concerned about them," Clint said. "I'm concerned they're going to weight us down."

Clint was starting to wonder if he could get Randall to help him lose a couple of Libbie's bags.

***

They went to the dining car for lunch, since they had all had light breakfasts. Libbie sat by the window and looked out at the passing scenery while they waited for their food.

"When George and I came west," she commented, "railroad travel was still fairly new. Now it's just common to be moving at these speeds."

"The faster the better, I suppose," Randall said. "It keeps the train robbers away." He looked at Clint. "Doesn't it?"

"Sure," Clint said, "unless they're already on board."

Randall looked around nervously.

The waiter came with their lunch, set the plates down and smiled at Libbie.

"Would the lady like anythin' else?" he asked.

"No, thank you," she said. "This looks fine."

The man nodded, turned and walked away. Clint noticed that he dropped the towel that was draped over his arm, and kept on going until he was out the door of the car—which seemed odd.

Libbie was lifting her sandwich to her mouth when Clint snapped, "Don't," and took it from her.

"What's wrong?"

He took the top piece of bread off the sandwich and examined the contents.

"There's more here than just chicken," he said.

"Onions?" she asked. "I told him no onions."

"No, not onions," Clint said, holding it out to show her. "Ground glass."

"What?" She looked shocked.

He dropped the sandwich onto the table and got to his feet.

"Send for the conductor," he told Randall, "and show it to him."

"Where are you going?" Randall called.

"I'm going to try to catch that phony waiter!"

***

The man had disappeared.

Clint went through the same door the imposter had gone through, and into the next car, which was the passenger car. But there was no sign of him. He wondered if the man had jumped off the train?

When he got back to the dining car, a conductor was apologizing profusely to Libbie.

"I don't know how this happened, Ma'am," he was saying.

"I told you how it happened," Randall said. "The waiter was a phony—here's Mr. Adams."

The conductor turned to face Clint as he reached them.

"You're Clint Adams?" he asked.

"That's right."

"I was tellin' the lady we're so sorry—"

"It's not your fault," Clint said, "unless you want to tell us how a phony got in here to impersonate a waiter?"

"Waiters are hired and fired all the time," the conductor said.

"By who?"

"No one on board," the man said. "It's done while we're in a station."

"I'd still like to talk to somebody—can you have all the waiters line up?" Clint asked. "Maybe one of them can describe the man who did this."

"Where would you like them?" the conductor asked.

"The kitchen will do."

"I'll come and get you when I have them all assembled," the man promised.

"That's fine."

"What about some food?" Libbie asked.

Clint looked at her.

"You're hungry?"

"Starved."

"I'll have something brought out," the conductor said. "Something safe."

Clint looked at Libbie, who raised her eyebrows at him.

"Do it!" Clint said.

Chapter Sixteen

When the conductor came for him, Clint left Libbie in the dining car with Randall, both of them waiting for food. He followed the man into the kitchen where four waiters were standing in line, as if at attention.

"This man is Clint Adams," the conductor said to them. "He has some questions for you. I'd advise you to answer truthfully."

He stepped aside.

"A phony waiter just served a woman a sandwich with ground glass in it," Clint said.

"What?" one waiter said. The others all looked surprised.

"Do any of you know who he was?"

The four waiters exchanged glances, then looked at Clint. Three of them shrugged and the fourth said, "We're the only four waiters working the train."

"There was a fifth," Clint said. "Somehow he got into this kitchen, got ahold of a sandwich, doctored it, delivered it, and disappeared."

The waiters all stared at him helplessly.

"Okay, tell me this," Clint said. "If you wanted to disappear, how would you do it?"

"Baggage car?" one waiter said.

"Stock car," another said.

"Jump off the train," a third said.

The fourth just looked puzzled.

Clint looked at the conductor.

"Do you have a security man on this train?"

"We do," the conductor said, "but he's supposed to stay out of sight. Nobody knows he's security."

"Well, I need to speak with him."

"I can bring him here," the conductor said.

"Do it." As the conductor left, Clint said to the waiters, "You can go back to work."

They all nodded and went to grab some plates.

One waiter came up to him and asked, "Are you hungry?"

"Starving, but I'll eat later."

The waiter looked around, then grabbed a sandwich from a plate of them and held it out to Clint.

"Here," he said. "No glass, I promise."

Clint accepted it. "Thanks." He bit into it. Chicken, no glass, as promised.

He was finishing the sandwich when the conductor returned with a man wearing a dark suit. He was portly, in his forties, with a heavy mustache.

"Mr. Adams?"

"That's right."

"Victor Lazlo, railroad security."

They shook hands.

"Has the conductor told you anything?"

"He has, but I'd rather hear it from you."

Clint told the man about riding the train with Libbie Custer, and about the sandwich she received with glass in it.

"The waiter immediately left the car, which is how I knew he was a phony. But when I followed, he was gone."

"He could've jumped off," Lazlo said.

"That's true, but I'd like to search the train, see if we can spot him."

"You'll know him if you see him?"

"I'll know him."

"Then let's go."

***

They did a thorough search of each car, including the baggage and stock cars.

"He could be outside, on top of one of the cars," Lazlo said.

"Okay, then," Clint said. "Outside."

Lazlo rubbed his belly.

"I'm not really built for climbing on top of the cars."

"I'll climb up to take a look," Clint said. "You just watch my back."

"That I can do," Lazlo promised.

Chapter Seventeen

Clint climbed down from atop the last car and said, "Nothing."

"Well, that's it, then," Lazlo said.

"There's no place else we can look?" Clint asked.

"Not that I know of," the security man said. "Unless you want to knock on the door of every sleeping car. And I'd have to get an okay for that from my boss."

"How do we do that?"

"Telegraph office at the next station."

"Well, we can do that and hope he's not in one of them right now, terrorizing a passenger."

Lazlo scowled.

"He could have jumped off the train, you know. Could be gone."

"He could be," Clint agreed. "How long is it until the next station?"

"Hours," Lazlo said.

"It's up to you, Mr. Lazlo," Clint said.

"Damn it," Lazlo swore. "Okay, let's do it."

***

The next hour was spent going from cabin to cabin, knocking, asking the occupants if they were all right or if they could come in and look around. As it turned out, nobody objected, and all the cabins were empty.

No phony waiter.

"What if—" Lazlo started, then stopped. "No, never mind."

"Go ahead," Clint said. "Say it."

"I was just thinking," Lazlo said, "what if he's one of the passengers. He put on a white coat, impersonated a waiter, did what he wanted, then went back to his seat."

"So you think he might be sitting in the passenger car even now."

"It's a thought."

"It's a good one," Clint admitted. "It seems he's either there, or jumped off, in which case he took a chance on breaking his leg or back, or even cracking his skull."

"You say you can recognize him," Lazlo reminded Clint. "Was he your waiter the entire time?"

"No," Clint said, "he brought Mrs. Custer her sandwich. That was it."

"And you saw him."

"For a moment."

"But you'd know him."

"I would."

"Then let's go have a look," Lazlo said. "This would seem to be our last chance."

They walked back through the dining car, where Libbie Custer and Lucius Randall still sat.

"Can we go back to our seats now?" she asked.

"No, not yet," Clint said. "We have one last place to look."

"Where?" Randall asked.

"Among the passengers in the next car," Clint said. "We think he might have simply taken off the white waiter's coat and sat in a seat."

"That would take courage," Libbie said.

"Or desperation," Lazlo said to her. "We were traveling too fast for him to jump off and land safely. This was his only out."

"Mr. Lazlo and I are going to have a look," Clint said. "Just wait here 'til we get back."

"What will you do if you find him?" Libbie asked.

"I think that will probably be up to him."

He and Lazlo continued on through the car, out the door and into the passenger car.

Chapter Eighteen

They stopped just inside the door. A few of the passengers turned to look, but for the most part they were being ignored.

"You go through first," Clint said, "and stop at the other door. If he's here, we'll have him boxed in."

"All right."

Lazlo strolled down the aisle amiably, and when he got to the other end he turned and stood in front of the door.

It was Clint's turn. He walked slowly, his eyes raking over each and every passenger. For those whose backs were to him, he had to glance back as he passed. It was one of these men whose face he recognized.

"You," Clint said.

"Me?" the man asked.

"Stand up."

"Why?" He was a young man, wearing a black suit and boiled white shirt, but earlier he had been wearing a waiter's white coat.

"Because I said so."

The man laughed, looked around at other passengers who were now watching both of them.

"And who are you?" he asked. "Why should I do anything you say?"

"That man is railroad security," Clint said, pointing at Lazlo. "Would you stand if he asked you to?"

"I paid my money," the man said. "I'm a passenger."

"This man," Clint said, pointing at him, "put on a white jacket, impersonated a waiter, and tried to give a woman a sandwich with broken glass in it."

Several women caught their breath.

"Why don't you tell them who that woman is?" the seated man asked. "Her name is Elizabeth Custer. She's the widow of George Armstrong Custer, the man who got all his men killed at the Little Bighorn. Why shouldn't I give her a glass sandwich?"

"Why should she pay for anything her husband did?" Clint asked.

"She defends him, doesn't she?" the man asked.

"He was her husband," Clint said. "She's loyal to his memory. You can't hold that against a woman. Now, stand up."

"No," the man said, "if you're gonna kill me, kill me while I'm sittin' here, in front of all these people."

"I don't have any intention of killing you," Clint said. "That is, unless you force me to."

"This man is Clint Adams," the man said, "the Gunsmith. He's gonna kill me."

There were some murmurs, and then a woman said, loudly and clearly, "If you put glass in a woman's sandwich, then perhaps he should kill you."

"Thank you, Ma'am," Clint said, then addressed the seated man again. "Come on, let's talk."

As the man moved to get up, Clint saw his left hand start to go behind his back.

"Don't—" he warned, but it was too late.

As the man came out with a gun in his hand, Clint drew and fired. The bullet struck the man in the thickest part of his body, slamming him back against his seat. Clint had shown the presence of mind to make sure that the bullet did not pass through him and strike the woman sitting with her back to him. In any event, she screamed and leaped forward, but she was fine.

Victor Lazlo came rushing over with his gun out, but the action was finished.

"Damn it," Clint said, "I wanted to find out who put him up to it."

"He didn't leave you much choice, did he?"

"No, he didn't."

The woman sitting with her back to the dead man was now leaning as far forward as she could, and was starting to make a high, keening noise.

"It's okay, Ma'am," Clint said. "You're okay."

"You could have killed me, you maniac!" the middle-aged woman snapped at him, her eyes flashing angrily.

"Ma'am, he didn't leave me much choice."

"You fired your gun in a crowded railroad car, you idiot!" She looked at Lazlo. "I insist you arrest this man for endangering our lives."

Lazlo looked at Clint.

"You go back to the dining car," the security man said. "I'll take care of this."

"Okay, thanks," Clint said.

"And send the conductor back, will you? Ask him to bring a couple of men to remove this body."

"Right."

As Clint started away, he heard the woman saying, "You're letting him go? I told you I wanted him arrested!"

"Ma'am," he heard Lazlo saying, "you've got entirely the wrong idea of what just happened."

"Do I?" She demanded, her voice a high squeak. "Do I really?"

"Ma'am," Lazlo told her, "you're going to have to settle down . . ."

Chapter Nineteen

Clint explained what happened to Libbie and Randall.

"Is it safe for her to sit in the passenger car?" Randall asked, nodding toward Libbie.

"I'll try to have the railroad security man stay there and watch."

"And where will you be?" she asked.

"They're moving the body to the stock car," Clint said. "I'm going to have a look at it, see if there's anything that can tell us who he was and why he did what he did."

"Perhaps," Libbie said, "he was the man who has been sending me the letters."

"Do you have any of the letters with you?" Clint asked.

"Why would you want those?"

"Just one," Clint said. "Maybe the man has something on him that will enable me to compare the handwriting."

"I see," Libbie said. "Yes, I have the letters with me. They're in my trunk."

"May I open the trunk and look for them?" Clint asked.

Yes, Mr. Adams," she said, "you may."

***

When Clint entered the stock car he saw the body laid out in an empty stall. Further toward the back he saw Eclipse, standing quietly.

A man turned and looked at him.

"Can I go back to work in the kitchen?" the man asked. "I'm not cut out for . . . this."

"Go ahead," Clint said.

"Thanks."

The man hurried from the car.

Clint crouched down next to the dead man and went through his pockets. There was nothing that could be used for a handwriting comparison. That meant there was no reason for him to go through Libbie Custer's trunk, which was off in a corner of the baggage car. Still, he did have her permission.

Clint walked over to Eclipse and put his hand on the Darley's neck.

"This dead man is telling no tale," he said. "Time to move on to the next car."

He left the stock car and entered the one holding the passengers' baggage. He found Libbie's trunk and, using the key she had entrusted to him, opened it.

He found the letters among other personal papers. Some were old letters from her husband. He did not read those. He looked at the threatening letters, invariably telling her that she would soon join her husband.

The only other things in the trunk were items of clothing—dresses, mostly, but some shirts and trousers. These were the clothes she would need for the trail. He considered tossing the dresses out the door, perhaps even the entire trunk, but decided against it.

He closed the trunk, and locked it.

***

Both Libbie Custer and Lucius Randall kept their eyes open and alert, studying the other passengers seated in the car. At the front stood Victor Lazlo, the railroad security man. He stepped aside as the door opened and Clint walked through it.

"Anything?" Lazlo asked.

"No," Clint said. "No indication why he did it. He had nothing in his pockets, at all."

"Well, that pretty much figures, doesn't it?" Lazlo asked. "No matter what happened, he wouldn't have wanted to be identified."

"No, you're right, he wouldn't," Clint said. "I'm going to sit with Mrs. Custer. You can return to your regular work, if you like."

"This is my work, Mr. Adams."

Clint nodded, and walked to where Libbie and Randall were seated.

"Well?" Libbie asked, as he sat next to her, across from Randall.

"Nothing," he said.

"And my trunk?"

Clint handed her the key.

"I had no need of it," he said. "The man had nothing in his pockets."

"So now what?" Libbie asked.

"Now we continue on, as planned," Clint said. "But at least we know that the letters you received were real, and serious. We'll be on the alert from here on."

She frowned.

"I suppose I was hoping they were just empty threats," she commented.

"We'll watch out for you, Ma'am," Randall said. "Clint and I."

"I know you will, Lucius."

She turned her head and went back to looking out the window.

Chapter Twenty

Clint and Randall carried Libbie Custer's luggage into the Austin House Hotel lobby. Randall then went to the front desk to secure their rooms, one for each of them.

The hotel had bell boys who assisted them in carrying Libbie's bags to her room.

"Get some rest," Clint told her. "We'll come back to take you to supper."

"When will we be leaving?" she asked.

"Not for a day or two," Clint said. "we have to outfit, which means getting you and Randall horses and saddles."

"Can I depend on you for that, or must I be there?" she asked.

"If you trust me to choose a horse for you, there's no reason for you to come along."

"I think I can leave that up to you," she said.

"Fine," Clint said, "but that'll be tomorrow. Will you eat with us tonight, or should I have something sent to your room?"

"I believe I'll dine with the two of you," Libbie said.

"Then we'll see you later."

Clint stepped out into the hall, where Randall was waiting.

"You gents are down here, sir," a bell boy said, and led the way. They had rooms right across from each other.

They each opened their doors, then turned and looked at the other.

"What's next?" Randall asked.

"Just relax," Clint said. "We'll go out and have some supper. No need to do anything until tomorrow morning. That's when you and I will go horse hunting."

"Suits me," Randall said. "Knock hard. I might be asleep now that I have a bed."

"Don't blame you," Clint said, and they both closed their doors.

***

Clint came awake with a start. He'd had no intention of falling asleep, but had reclined on the bed just for a moment. A check of the time told him he'd been out for an hour.

He got up, washed his face in the basin on the dresser, then went across the hall and knocked on Randall's door. He had to do it several times before the young man answered, looking groggy.

"Wow, I was out," Randall said.

"Get yourself around and meet me at Libbie's room," Clint said.

"Right," Randall said, through a yawn, and closed the door.

Clint walked down the hall, knocked on Libbie's door. She answered immediately, looking impossibly fresh in a clean shirt and skirt.

"It's about time," she said. "I've been ready for a while." She looked into the hall. "Where's Lucius?"

"He'll be along," Clint said.

"I've been looking out the window," she said. "Austin has changed. It's much more . . . metropolitan than it was when George and I came through."

"We'll eat here in the hotel," Clint said. "I don't want to take any chances on the street."

"You're thinking someone might take a shot at you?" she asked. "Because of your reputation?"

"That's always a possibility," he admitted, "but I was thinking about you."

"Oh," she said, as if it were a sobering thought that someone might take a shot at her.

At that point Randall came walking down the hall, still looking sleepy.

"All right," Clint said, "let's go."

They went down to the lobby, across it to the dining-room entrance. Clint asked for a table near the back.

"Why can't we sit in front, by the window?" Libbie asked him.

"For the same reason we're not out there walking the streets."

As they sat she asked, "What's going to happen when we're on the trail? Anyone could shoot us from ambush."

"They could," Clint said, "but at least we won't have to watch for people in windows, alleys, or on rooftops."

"All I'm trying to do is remember my husband," she said. "What's so bad about that?"

"With your book, you're trying to get people to remember the Custer you know," Clint said. "That's not going to happen. The Little Bighorn was a catastrophe that could have been avoided."

"He was following orders!"

"I doubt anyone ordered your husband to take on an opposing force ten times the size of his."

"You weren't there!" she snapped.

"You're right about that," Clint said. "I'm just suggesting you could have stayed home and had very nice memories of your husband. Instead, you're out here trying to shove that memory down people's throats."

She glared at Clint, but before she could say anything else Randall asked, "How about steak?"

Chapter Twenty-One

After the meal Libbie insisted on returning to her room, alone. She had said very little while eating.

"You two just don't get along," Randall said, as she left the table.

"We have different opinions, is all," Clint said. "She sees Custer through the eyes of love."

"And you?"

Clint laughed.

"No love there," he said, "just cold, hard facts."

"So he really wasn't a good officer?" Randall asked.

"He was a terrible officer."

"And why was that?"

"Too much ego," Clint said. "He thought he knew better than everyone, and anyone."

"And he didn't."

"He always had more experienced sergeants under his command," Clint observed. "All he had to do was be guided by them."

"And he'd still be alive?"

"Maybe."

"You'd think she'd prefer that," Randall said. "All he had to do was ask questions, and she'd still have him."

"You'll never convince her of that," Clint said.

"I'd never try," Randall said, "but you . . ."

"Yes?"

"You seem intent on provoking her."

"Do I?" Clint said. "I think I'm intent on speaking the truth. I won't tell anyone that George Armstrong Custer was a hero when I know he wasn't."

"Then it would seem to me you'd be better off not talking about him, at all."

"Little chance of that, given why we're here," Clint said.

"Sir?" the waiter asked. "Dessert?"

"How about some pie?" Clint said to Randall.

The younger man turned to the waiter and asked, "Do you have apple?"

***

After washing down slices of apple pie with a pot of coffee, Clint paid the bill and they left.

"What now?" Randall asked.

"A drink?"

Randall looked across the lobby at the entrance to the hotel's bar.

"Not there," Clint said. "Let's take a walk and see what we find."

"What about Mrs. Custer?"

"She'll be fine for the moment," Clint said. "As long as she doesn't bite into any more glass sandwiches."

***

They walked a few blocks and found a saloon called The Going Concern Saloon.

"Clever," Randall said, looking in the window, "and it looks accurate."

"Let's have a closer look."

They went inside and, for a change, when the Gunsmith entered a saloon, he didn't draw very much attention. They went to the bar and found room for themselves.

"Two beers," Clint told the bartender.

"Comin' up."

They looked around, didn't see any sign of gambling. But there were plenty of girls working the floor, carrying drinks and dodging grasping hands. In the front of the room was a piano, next to a stage.

"Any entertainment tonight?" Clint asked, as the bartender served them.

"No," the man said. "We don't got no piano player. The one we had got shot last week. We'll probably have one by the end of the week."

Clint nodded. That wouldn't matter to them. They'd be gone by then.

They turned back to the bar, gave the mugs of beer their attention.

"We'll get an early start in the morning," Clint said, "find you and Libbie your outfits. After that, we'll have to pick up some supplies."

"And when will we be underway?"

"The next morning," Clint said.

"Where to?"

"A place called Hempstead."

"Hempstead?"

"How much of what's in Libbie's book do you know?" Clint asked. "Or her future book."

"Nothing."

"You work for the publisher."

"That doesn't mean I ever read the book," Randall said. "To do my job, there was no need."

"I see," Clint said. "Well, then maybe I should tell you a little bit about Hempstead, Texas."

Chapter Twenty-Two

"In eighteen sixty-six, General Phil Sherman sent Custer to Texas with a thousand men. Even though Lee had surrendered at Appomattox, Texas continued to fight. The war didn't end here for at least another month. Custer was sent to be sure that it did, though."

"And he succeeded?"

"He did, but the way he did it . . . I doubt that Libbie is going to write about the way it actually happened."

"Which was?"

"Custer had a certain way of . . . punishing those who didn't do as they were told."

"And how was that?"

"He gave them twenty-five lashes, and shaved their head."

"Jesus."

"And he visited that discipline upon his own men, as well," Clint went on.

"But . . . why?"

"To dissuade them from looting."

"And Mrs. Custer knows all this?"

"I'm sure she does."

"And she still defends him?"

"Possibly," Clint said, "she agreed with his tactics, at the time. Remember, she was here with him."

"Do you really think an army officer discussed his tactics with his wife?"

"I think they were pretty close, which was why he took her with him everywhere he went."

"Hempstead?"

"As I remember, they spent a couple of months in Hempstead, but most of their time in Texas was spent here. Custer liked giving his wife some creature comforts, like a bathtub, a fireplace and a social life."

"She does seem that type," Randall said, "except she's going to be on the trail with us."

"Not for long," Clint said, "at least, not here. She'll want to look at Austin and Hempstead, and then move on, I'm sure."

"To where?"

"That'll be up to her, but I know they spent some time in Kansas."

"What about the Little Bighorn?" Randall asked. "Is she going to want to go there?"

"I don't know if she's writing about that," Clint said. "At least, not in this book."

"I'm sure Mr. McMay would love for her to write about it," Randall said, "but how can she defend that?"

"I think she could find a way," Clint said.

They finished their beers and walked back to their hotel.

"Meet me in the lobby for breakfast," Clint said, as they reached the doors to their rooms, "and then we'll go look at some horses."

"What time?"

"Early."

"First light?"

"Not that early."

***

A half hour later, Clint had removed his boots, unbuttoned his shirt, and reclined on the bed with a Jules Verne book. When the knock came at the door, he grabbed his gun and padded softly to it, pressing his ear.

"Who is it?"

He expected either Libbie Custer or Randall, but a male voice said, "Mr. Adams, it's the desk clerk. I have a message for you."

"Slide it under the door," Clint said.

"Yessir."

Clint looked down, saw a slip of paper appear.

"I'll come down and give you a tip in the morning," Clint said.

"No need, sir," the man said. "Have a pleasant evening."

Clint waited until he heard the man's footsteps retreat, then bent over and picked up the piece of paper.

He unfolded it and saw a note asking him to come down to the bar for a talk. It was signed VIRGINIA GRAY, JOURNALIST.

It was most likely a woman who had heard that he was in town, possibly with Libbie Custer, and she wanted an interview. He had to admit, if the note had come from a man, he would have ignored it. But he thought he should go down, hear what she had to say, and let her down easy. Or refer her to Henry McMay and let her talk with him, albeit by telegraph.

He pulled his boots on, buttoned his shirt, strapped on his gun, and left the room.

***

He stopped at the front desk to give the clerk the tip he promised, and to get a description of the lady journalist.

"She's quite pretty, sir," the middle-aged clerk said, "with brown hair, wearing a very business-like suit."

"Do you know her?" Clint asked. "Is she local?"

"She is," the clerk said. "She writes for the *Austin Journal*. The newspaper has a regular table in our dining-room, and in the bar."

"Okay, thanks," Clint said, and headed for the bar.

Chapter Twenty-Three

As he entered the bar, he looked around. It was late, but plenty of the tables were still taken, as well as spots at the bar. But he only saw one woman seated alone, and she matched the description from the desk clerk.

He walked over and asked, "Miss Gray?"

She looked up at him and smiled.

"Mr. Adams?"

"That's right."

"I wasn't sure you'd come down."

"Well, you were kind enough to send a message up instead of knocking on the door, yourself."

She stood up and shook his hand. Her grip was firm for someone fairly young and not very large. He figured her for under thirty.

"Please, have a seat," she said. "Can I get you a drink?"

"Yes, I'll have a beer."

As they sat, she waved at the bartender. He brought over a beer and nodded to her.

"I understand this is your regular table," Clint said.

"Not mine," she said. "The newspaper's. I get to use it as long as I work for the Journal."

"And just what do you do for the Journal?"

"I write," she said. "I do stories about people."

"I don't do interviews."

"I'm afraid you're not the one I'm interested in interviewing, Mr. Adams."

"Ah," he said, "Mrs. Custer."

"Yes."

"Why not contact her publisher?" he asked. "I'm sure they'd be happy to set something up."

"It would take too long," she said, "too many telegrams. When I heard you were here with her, I thought I'd ask for your help."

"I can't make her talk to you."

"But you can ask her for me," Virginia Gray said. "Make a request."

"I could do that."

"The question is, will you?"

"Why not?" he asked. "One of the reasons she's here is to promote her work, isn't it?"

"That's what I was assuming."

"Then I don't see why she wouldn't talk with you."

"So you'll ask her?"

"I'll ask her to meet you," he said. "Then you can ask her yourself."

"That sounds good. When?"

"At breakfast tomorrow," he said. "If she agrees, I'll bring her to your newspaper's office. There you can talk to her while I'm busy outfitting us."

"You'll be going to Hempstead?"

"Yes," he said. "How'd you know?"

"I do my research," she said.

He noticed how pale and smooth her skin was. Apparently, she did her research inside, away from the sun.

"Did you know Custer?" she asked.

"I did."

"So is that why you're here?" she asked. "To help her with her book, to tell their story?"

"I don't give a shit about their story," he said. "I'm here to insure nothing happens to her while she's doing *her* research."

"It doesn't sound like you and Custer were friends."

"We had a mutual dislike for each other."

"And respect?" she asked.

He stared at her and said, "Dislike."

***

After they finished their drink, he walked her out to the lobby, and to the front door.

"Thank you for coming down," she said. "You had no idea who I was."

"I asked the desk clerk," he told her. "I was fairly certain you weren't someone waiting to bushwhack me."

She smiled, which turned her face from pretty to beautiful.

"Perhaps before you leave Austin, you'll allow me to buy you a steak," she said. "We have great steaks here."

"That sounds good," Clint said. "We'll be leaving day after tomorrow, but I believe we'll be back soon."

"Good," she said. "I'll look forward to it. And I look forward to hearing from you tomorrow."

He watched her walk out the front door and speak to the doorman. Then she turned and waved to him.

***

Back in his room, Clint thought that being interviewed by Virginia Gray would be just what Libbie Custer wanted. It would give her another opportunity to do what she loved best, talk about her husband.

The soldier.

The officer.

The hero.

Bullshit!

Chapter Twenty-Four

"Is she going to come down for breakfast?" Randall asked, when they met in the lobby the next morning.

"I don't know," Clint said. "Why don't you go on up and knock on her door?"

"She was kind of mad yesterday," Randall said. "I think I'll pass."

"Then let's go and eat," Clint said.

"What about the newspaper lady?" Randall asked. "You told her you'd ask Mrs. Custer this morning."

"If she comes down," Clint said, "I will."

They ordered and were halfway through their meal when Libbie appeared.

"Sorry I'm late," she said, seating herself. "I'm happy to see you didn't let that stop you from eating."

"We didn't think you were coming down, at all," Clint said.

"Why? Because we disagreed yesterday? We are going to disagree many more times, and yet have to travel together, eat together."

The waiter came over and she ordered.

"What's on the agenda for today?" she asked.

"Horses," Randall said.

"More than that," Clint said. "We need to outfit ourselves. That means horses, saddles, supplies, ammunition."

"Ammunition?" she asked. "You're expecting trouble? From where? Indians?"

"I'm always expecting trouble, Mrs. Custer," Clint said. "And I'm always ready for it. That's why I'm still alive."

"I understand."

"But there is something you might want to do today," Clint said.

He explained about his meeting with Virginia Gray, and her desire to interview Elizabeth Custer.

"You can talk about your husband, your book, and your next book," he finished. "That's what McMay would want you to do, isn't it?"

"Indeed," Libbie said. "And it's what I want to do. I'll go over there after we eat."

"We'll take you," Clint said, "and leave you there while we go to a livery. Then we'll come back and get you, and we can all go to a mercantile for supplies."

"All right," she agreed.

"But eat," Clint said, "and take your time. There's no rush."

***

They took a cab from the front of the hotel to the office of the *Austin Journal*. There he introduced Libbie to Virginia Gray, who in turn introduced all of them to her editor, a man named Rackam. He was a white-haired man in his sixties, with fingertips permanently stained black.

"Mr. Adams," Rackam said, "ma'am." He executed a clumsy little bow to Libbie. "Thank you for agreeing to this."

"It's my pleasure, Mr. Rackam," Libbie said, "but it was my understanding that I would be speaking with the lady."

"I believe this is too important a thing," the editor said. "I've decided I should do it."

Clint could see that this did not sit well with Virginia Gray. Her jaw was set, and a muscle was jumping.

Libbie saw it to.

"No," she said.

"I beg your pardon?" Rackam asked.

"The agreement was that I would talk to Miss Gray," Libbie said. "That's why I'm here. To talk with her."

"But—"

"If not," Libbie said, "then we'll be going."

As she turned the man said, "No, wait!"

She stopped.

"All right," he said, "okay, since that's what you agreed to."

Libbie turned to Clint.

"I'll be fine now," she said. "Go and get your horses."

"*Our* horses," Clint corrected.

When he and Randall left, Libbie had already sat down with Virginia Gray, and started talking.

***

After disembarking from the train, Clint had taken Eclipse to the livery closest to the station. While he examined it and found it fitting, he also noticed that they sold horses, saddles, saddlebags and blankets. So that was the first place they went.

"Checkin' on your horse?" the hostler asked. "I'm takin' good care of 'im."

"I'm sure you are," Clint said. "No, we need to be outfitted for two more riders."

"Everythin'?" the man asked. "Saddlebags, canteens, blankets and the like?"

"Yes."

"And you can pay?"

"Oh, yes."

The man grinned.

"Excellent. Let's do some business. Whiskey?"

Chapter Twenty-Five

They had one glass of whiskey each and then got down to it.

The horses were in a corral out back. Clint and Randall accompanied the man there, and Randall kept quiet while Clint dickered.

Clint made a deal for a five-year-old mare, a six-year-old gelding, two saddles complete with saddlebags, blankets and canteens. The dickering did not go on very long, as Clint wasn't spending his own money.

"We'll pick them up tomorrow morning," he said, when they were done.

"They'll be ready."

"Where's the best place to buy some supplies?" Clint asked, while settling the bill.

"Two blocks over is Sloan's General Store. Might not be the best, but it's close and it's as good as any."

"Thanks," Clint said. "We'll see you tomorrow."

Clint and Randall left the livery and started following the simple directions to the general store.

"You didn't get a receipt," Randall said.

"What?"

"Mr. McMay's going to want your receipts."

"You're my witness," Clint said. "You can tell him how much I spent."

When they reached the general store, Clint saw that it was small, but as soon as he entered, he knew it had what they needed.

"Are we going to buy so much that we'll need a pack animal?" Randall asked.

"No," Clint said, "pack animals just slow us down. Whatever we buy, we'll split into three gunny sacks, and we'll each have one hanging from our saddle pommels."

"That makes sense," Randall said.

Rather than walk around, grabbing items off shelves, he left it to the clerk to collect the things they wanted. Once they were piled on the counter, the man began counting up the items.

When he handed Clint the tally, it was paid without question.

"Do you have animals, or a buckboard?" the man asked.

"No," Clint said, "just divide the supplies evenly among three gunny sacks. We'll pick it all up in the morning."

"It'll be ready."

Clint nodded, left the store with Randall.

"Now what?"

"Let's go and see if Libbie is finished with the newspaper lady."

***

As they entered the office of *The Austin Journal* both Libbie and Virginia looked up at them from their seated positions. The editor was nowhere to be seen.

"Are you finished?" Clint asked.

"Just now," Virginia said, standing. "Thank you for putting us together."

"Are you ready to go?" Clint asked Libbie.

"Yes," she said, also standing, "but there is another place I wish to visit."

"Why not?" Clint asked. "We're outfitted, and our supplies are waiting for us. We have the rest of the day ahead of us."

Libbie turned to Virginia.

"Thank you for listening," she said.

"Thank you for talking to me."

She left the office with Clint and Randall.

"Where to?" Clint asked.

"The outskirts of town," she said. "Get us a cab. I'll tell him where."

***

They waved down a cab drawn by a single horse, and Libbie gave him her directions. When they stopped in front of the large building, Clint stared up at it.

"This is the old Blind Asylum building," the driver said. "It's abandoned now."

Clint stepped down, helped Libbie down. She stood there staring at the building.

"This was where we lived when we were stationed here," she said. "After we left Hempstead."

"Do you want to go inside?"

She shook her head.

"It would just be depressing."

"And Hempstead?" Clint asked. "Do you still want to go there?"

"Yes." She looked at him. "As depressing as that will also be, yes. Can we leave tomorrow morning?"

"We're ready," he said.

"Good," she said. "Then we might as well go back to the hotel."

He helped her back up into the cab, where she sat next to Randall.

"You lived here?" Randall asked, eyeing the two-story building.

"Once upon a time," she said, "when life was different."

Clint climbed into the cab and said to the driver, "Let's go."

Chapter Twenty-Six

The next morning they left Austin, heading for Hempstead. It was there that General Custer had put his cruel and unusual punishments into effect.

Clint still didn't know whether or not Libbie Custer knew about these things, but he didn't think it was the right time to ask. They hadn't had an argument in at least a day, and he wanted to keep it that way, for now.

Hempstead was over a hundred miles from Austin. If he rode Eclipse hard, he could do it in two days. With Randall along, it would be three. But because Libbie was with them, he settled for four.

They camped the first night, and Libbie pitched in. While Clint cared for the horses, Randall collected wood and made a fire. After that, Libbie cooked.

As Clint and Randall came to the fire, she handed them each a plate of bacon-and-beans, and a mug of coffee.

"It's been a while since I've had trail food," she admitted.

"If this is trail food," Randall said, "it isn't half bad."

Clint didn't bother telling Randall that some nights on the trail meant coffee and beef jerky or, in the case of a cold camp, just jerky and water.

When they were done, Libbie cleaned off the utensils and stowed them away before rolling herself up in her bedroll.

"We're going to split the watch," Clint told Randall.

"Watch?" Randall asked. "For what?"

"I don't think that glass sandwich is going to be the only attempt at dissuading Libbie from writing her second book."

Randall looked around.

"You mean somebody's following us?"

"I don't know," Clint said. "But I don't want any surprises. Have you ever stood watch before?"

"No," Randall said. "There's not much call for it in publishing."

Clint gave the young man a quick course in watching and listening, to what was out there and in camp.

"Eclipse will let you know when he hears something."

"Your horse can do that?" Randall asked.

"His ears have saved my life more than once," Clint said.

He also explained to Randall about night vision, and not staring into the fire.

"Do you want to go first or second?" he then asked.

"I'll go first," Randall said.

"Wake me if you have any problems," Clint said. "And keep the coffee pot going."

"My coffee skills are awful."

"Just toss a handful into the pot and forget about it," Clint said. "That's all it takes."

"Okay."

"And here." Clint handed Randall his rifle. "Keep this across your knees."

"How come we didn't buy me my own gun?" Randall asked.

"I think my rifle will do you for now," Clint said. "If we decide we need to get you your own gun, we can do that later."

Clint had set his saddle and bedroll down across the camp from Libbie. He was keeping his distance because their opinions of her husband were so disparate, he didn't want to have any unnecessary conversations with her. That meant keeping some distance between them, at least until they got things worked out.

He settled down into his bedroll, with his holster rolled up and on the ground next to him.

***

When he woke, he laid still a moment and listened. What had awakened him?

"Clint." He heard Randall's voice.

"I'm awake," Clint said.

"I heard something," Randall said.

"So did I."

He crawled out of his bedroll, grabbed his holster and got to his feet, strapping it on.

"How long was I asleep?"

"About three hours," Randall said. "I was going to wake you in an hour."

Clint looked over at Eclipse, who was standing silently.

"He didn't make a sound?"

"No," Randall said. "That's why, at first, I thought I was wrong."

"No," Clint said, "I heard something, too, and it woke me up."

"What's going on?" Libbie asked, from her bedroll.

"Shh," Clint said. "We both heard something."

"Of course you did," Libbie said, lowering her voice. "There are all kinds of critters out there."

She stood up and came to join them by the fire. They poured some coffee and listened.

"I don't hear anything," she whispered.

"Somebody's out there," Clint said, "and they're watching us."

"How can you tell?" Libbie asked.

"I can feel it."

"George used to say that."

"Did he," Clint said, knowing he dared not say more.

How had Custer not "felt" the presence of two thousand Lakota, Northern Cheyenne, and Arapaho led by Crazy Horse and Chief Gall at the Little Bighorn?

Chapter Twenty-Seven

Clint remained awake 'til morning, told Randall and Libbie to go to sleep.

"Whoever they are," he said, "they're not coming in."

"How can you be sure?" Randall asked.

"I can't," Clint said, "that's why I'm staying awake, but it's what I feel."

He hoped Libbie wouldn't again comment on how that was what George used to say, and thankfully she didn't. Clint sure as hell didn't want his instincts being compared to those of George Armstrong Custer.

By first light, Clint had some bacon in the pan and a fresh pot of coffee going. The smell woke both Randall and Libbie.

"Hear anything else?" Randall asked, rubbing his face with both hands.

"Nothing," Clint said. "He was being very quiet."

Libbie accepted a cup of coffee from Clint with a nod of thanks. Then he divvied out the bacon and handed them each a plate.

"Will you go looking for him now that it's daylight?" Randall asked.

"No," Clint said, "let him follow. We'll see how far he wants to go."

"What if there's more than one?" Libbie asked.

"So far there doesn't seem to be," Clint said. "There would have been more noise if there were."

They broke camp, saddled the three horses and mounted up.

"How many more days to Hempstead?" Libbie asked.

"We may need to camp three more nights," Clint said. "If we push it, maybe two."

"Let's push it," she suggested.

Clint nodded, and they started off.

***

On the third morning Clint said, "We'll be there before dark."

"Are we still being followed?" Libbie asked.

"Yes," Clint said.

"Why don't you ride back and see who it is, while Lucius and I continue on."

"Because that might be what someone is waiting for me to do."

She stared across the fire at him.

"So you do think there are more than one?"

"I think he's been following us, not coming any closer, for days, for a reason. The only thing I can figure is it's to lure me out, and away from you."

"So they can do . . . what? Kill me?"

"Who knows?" Clint asked. "The glass in your sandwich may have been meant to harm you, or kill you. We have no way of knowing."

"Then why not let it happen?" she asked.

"What?"

"Ride out," she said, "let them think they've lured you away. Then you can also watch us at a distance, and wait to see what happens."

"Then if someone intercepts the two of you," he said. "I'll be too far away to be of assistance."

"What if you were within rifle distance?" she asked.

"I'd have to leave the two of you unarmed."

"You can't leave Lucius your pistol?"

"I'm useless with a pistol," Randall said.

"Let's stay with my plan," Clint said.

"Which is?" Libbie asked.

"To get you to Hempstead," Clint said. "We'll deal with whatever we find there."

"Very well," she said. "You're in charge."

Clint was surprised to hear those words come from her lips.

They broke camp for the final time and headed out.

***

"There it is," Clint said. "Hempstead."

Libbie stared ahead.

"It's bigger than it was when we were here," she commented.

"I figured that would be the case," Clint said. "Either that, or it would be gone."

"Certainly doesn't look gone," Randall said.

As they rode into Hempstead, they saw the recently constructed buildings, the new businesses, the fairly clean streets.

"This is all recent," Randall said.

"Obviously," Libbie said.

"My point is," Randall said, "it's not only grown since you were here last, but in the past few months."

"Let's get a hotel," Clint said, "and see to our horses, before we discuss the town's growth spurt, okay?"

"Sure," Randall said.

"Agreed," Libbie said.

"Let's take that one," Clint said, pointing to a hotel up ahead.

"Why that one?" Randall asked.

"Because," Clint said, "it's the first one we came to."

Chapter Twenty-Eight

They got three rooms at the Hotel Del Mar, then while Libbie went to hers, Clint and Randall took the horses to a livery.

"She doesn't look so happy to be here," Randall said, as they walked.

"Why would she be?" Clint asked. "Everything she's doing, and seeing, is reminding her of her husband."

"Why is that a bad thing?"

"Because he's dead."

"But . . . she likes talking about him, writing about him," Randall argued.

"I have a theory about that."

"What is it?"

"Guilt," Clint said. "She has to talk about him because she feels guilty if she doesn't. It would be like a betrayal."

"Then do you think she knows he wasn't the great soldier she claims he was?"

"No," Clint said, "I think she's managed to convince herself of that."

"But how?"

"Custer believed it of himself," Clint said, "and he convinced her."

"Jesus," Randall said. "then he was lying to both of them."

"Not really," Clint said. "His ego was so big that he actually believed it."

They found a livery and after Clint approved of it, left their horses in the care of the hostler who—predictably—was impressed by Eclipse.

"I'll take good care of him," he promised.

"All three," Clint said. "Take good care of all three of them."

"Right."

Clint and Randall removed their saddlebags, and Libbie's, Clint's rifle, and headed back to the hotel. Along the way they got closer looks at some of the new businesses that had obviously opened recently.

"That's an ice cream parlor," Randall said, pointing. "Out here?"

"The world is getting smaller every year, Lucius," Clint said.

"An Apothecary?" Randall asked, pointing.

"It's a growing town," Clint said. "Let's accept that."

"Yes, all right," Randall said.

***

When they got back to the Del Mar, they each went to their own room. The hotel may have been recently constructed, but there was still no indoor plumbing. There was a pitcher-and-basin on the chest of drawers, and a piss pot under the bed. And the clerk had informed them that there were several outhouses behind the building.

Clint washed his hands and face, changed his shirt, left his room and walked to Libbie's door.

"Are you hungry?" he asked, when she opened it.

"Yes."

Down the hall a door opened and Randall stepped out. When he saw them he hurried over.

"Real food?" he asked.

"After only three days you're tired of trail food?" Clint asked.

"I'm afraid so."

"Then yes," Clint said, "let's go and find some real food."

They had passed several cafes along the way between the hotel and the livery, so they chose one and entered. Getting a table against the back wall proved no problem, as they were between lunch and supper.

As they sat, Randall asked Libbie, "Will we be looking at the house you and the General stayed in while you were here?"

"No."

"Oh? Why not?"

"Because we lived in a tent," Libbie said. "None of this was here back then."

"None of it?"

"A few buildings," Libbie said. "That was all. And an Army camp. If you think trail food is bad, you should try Army chow. That was why I was so happy when we got back to Austin. I was able to sit at a real table, sleep in a real bed, and eat real food."

"I can understand that," Randall said.

Clint gave him a long look.

"After three days on the trail?"

"My first three days on the trail," the younger man pointed out.

When the waiter came over, Clint said, "You better get this young man what he wants quickly."

"Sir?" the waiter said.

"Steak," Randall said. "With all the trimmings."

"Make it two," Libbie said.

"Three," Clint chimed in.

Chapter Twenty-Nine

Libbie didn't talk while she ate.

"So tell me," Clint said, at one point, "if there's no house here, no memories, why are we here?"

She stared across the table at him, and for a moment he thought she wasn't going to answer.

"I just wanted to get a look at it," she said. "See how it changed."

"And?" Randall asked.

"It's changed a lot."

"Like most places and people do," Clint said.

"When people change, it's day by day," she said. "I wanted to see the way this place changed."

Clint and Randall waited, as it seemed she wasn't finished.

She looked down at her plate and said, "To tell the truth, I think I was hoping it would be . . . gone." She looked at them. "Wiped from the face of the earth."

Obviously, the time she had spent there was not good.

They finished their meals and the waiter asked about dessert.

"Maybe pie?" he asked.

"Not for me," she said, standing up, "but you boys stay and indulge. I want to go for a walk."

"Not without us," Clint said. To the waiter he said, "No pie."

They stepped outside.

"This isn't necessary, you know," she said.

"I think it is," Clint said. "We still don't know who was following us, and who was responsible for the glass in your sandwich."

"He's right," Randall said. "You're not going any-where without us."

"Lucius," she said, smiling at him, "you're worried about me?"

"Sure, I am," he said. "Mr. McMay would kill me if anything happened to you before you could write another book."

"I'm touched," she said, "really. Okay, gents, then let's walk."

They proceeded with Libbie Custer walking between them. One of them moved only when they had to allow someone to pass by, rather than making the citizens of the town move to accommodate them.

"What a difference," she commented, at one point.

"You said," Randall replied, "it's bigger."

"Not just the size," she said. "The feel."

When they reached one end of town she said, "I want to keep going."

"Where?" Clint asked.

"You'll see."

So they kept walking, leaving the town limits, and the road, behind.

Clint kept his eyes active, darting left and right, behind and ahead, still wondering about their tail on the road, and what their plans were.

They came to a clearing, where Libbie suddenly stopped and pointed.

"There," she said.

"What?" Randall asked. "What was there?"

"That's where we were billeted, George and I."

"How can you tell?" Randall asked. "The area's changed so much."

"Not that horizon," she said, pointing further out. "I stared out at it for two months, so it's been burned into my memory. This is where our tent was."

She walked a bit further, looking at the ground, then stopped, turned and faced them.

"My chair used to sit right here," she said. "While George was doing his duty, I would sit here and stare, sometimes sew or knit, like a good wife. Then he'd come back and we would have supper together. And talk about his day."

Clint looked at Randall, who understood the look.

"Did he tell you everything about his day?" the younger man asked.

"He told me what he could."

"What about his . . . methods of discipline?" Randall asked. "Did he discuss that with you?"

She looked at Clint, as if she understood that the questions were actually coming from him.

"No," she said, "he did not discuss his methods with me. He was in command, totally."

She looked out at the horizon again, then abruptly said, "I'm done here. We should go back."

"To the hotel?" Randall said.

"To Austin," she said. "I'm finished with Texas."

"Then where will we be going next?" Clint asked.

They started back to town.

"After the Civil War we were assigned two places before George was finally put in charge of the Seventh Cavalry," she said. "One was here, in Texas."

"And the other?" Randall asked,

"I believe Mr. Adams knows the answer to that," she said.

Randall looked at Clint, who said, "Kansas."

Chapter Thirty

They could not set out immediately for Austin. They had to spend one night in Hempstead, and leave in the morning.

"Do you want to eat with us later?" Clint asked, as they entered the hotel.

"I don't think so," she said. "Do you think you could bring something to my room?" She was looking at Randall.

"Uh, yes, of course," he said. "I'd be happy to. What would you like?"

"Whatever you two eat," she said, "will be fine."

She went up to her room, unwatched by the several people who were in the lobby. They also didn't look at Clint or Randall.

"Outside," Clint said.

They stepped out and Randall asked, "are we going for a drink?"

"No," Clint said, "we're going around back and using the rear door to get into the hotel."

"Why?"

"Those people in the lobby," Clint said. "They were minding their own business too deliberately."

***

They found an alley that led to the back of the hotel, found the back door and forced it.

"What do you think they're doing?" Randall asked.

"Right now they're probably going up to Libbie's room," Clint guessed.

"How many?"

"Two men and a woman."

"A woman?"

"Women disliked Custer as much as men did," Clint said.

"As much as you disliked him?"

"I didn't dislike Custer," Clint said. "I hated him."

They made their way up the back stairs, got to the hall in time to see the two men and woman force their way into Libbie Custer's room.

"Let's go."

"Do I need a gun?" Randall asked, as he followed Clint down the hall.

"No!"

When they got to the door, Clint leaned against it and listened.

"—the hell you think you're doing?" Libbie was saying.

"You're not who you think you are, and neither was your husband," a woman's voice said.

"What do you know about my husband?"

"We know he wasn't what he pretended to be," a man said.

"You don't know anything!"

"That's enough," the woman said. "We have to get her out of here."

"I'm not going anywhere with you," Libbie said, defiantly.

"Let's get her out of here before they come back!" the woman ordered, obviously in charge.

"Stay behind me," Clint whispered.

He backed up, kicked the door open and darted into the room, drawing his gun.

The three strangers all turned. When they saw him, the men went for their guns. The woman just stared.

Clint fired twice, hitting both men square in the chest. They both crumpled to the floor. He then turned his gun on the woman.

"No, wait, wait!" she screamed, holding her hands out in front of her.

From behind her, Libbie reached out, grabbed her shoulder, turned her around and hit her in the face with the water pitcher.

"Aaaaaah!" Libbie screamed, as the woman went down.

"Damn it!" Clint swore.

He knew, watching the woman go limp and fall, that she was dead before she hit the floor. He checked anyway, and also checked the fallen men.

"Are they dead?" Randall asked.

"Yes." He looked at Libbie. "I wanted one of them alive, preferably the woman.

"She's dead?" Libbie asked, shocked. "I . . . didn't mean to kill her. I was just . . . angry."

They heard some commotion in the hallway.

"Close that door!" he snapped at Randall. "We're going to have to deal with the law, now. So quickly, tell me what happened."

"There was a knock at the door. I thought it was you, so I opened it. They . . . forced their way in and started berating me. They were actually going to try to take me with them."

"Where?"

"They didn't say." She sat down on the bed and looked at her hands, which were shaking. "I need a drink."

"We'll get you one," Clint said. "After."

"After what?"

At that point there was a knock at the door and a man shouted, "This is the Sheriff! Open up!"

"After that," Clint said.

Chapter Thirty-One

"Sheriff Dan Farrell," the man said, after they had let him in.

"Clint Adams. That is Lucius Randall, and the lady is Mrs. Elizabeth Custer."

"Ah," the sheriff said, "the General's widow." The lawman—a man in his forties, wearing a badge that had seen better days—looked around at the bodies on the floor. "You killed them?"

"Yes," Clint said.

"No," Libbie said. "He killed those two men. I killed her." She pointed at the woman.

"What were they doin' here?" the lawman asked.

"They intended to kidnap me."

"Why?"

"I believe they wanted my publisher to withdraw my book from circulation," Libbie said. "And to keep me from writing another."

"Is that why you're here?" the sheriff asked.

"Yes," she said. "I'm collecting research for a second book."

The lawman looked around at the dead bodies again.

"How much longer do you intend to be in town?" he asked.

"'Til morning," Clint said. "Then we head back to Austin."

"That's good to hear," Farrell said. "I'll have these bodies removed."

"I'd like Mrs. Custer to have another room," Clint said.

"I'll talk to the desk clerk. It'll get done."

"Lucius," Clint said, "take Libbie to your room. Take my rifle."

"Yes, sir."

Randall opened the door and walked Libbie out into the hall, which had been cleared. That left Clint and the sheriff in the room with the three bodies.

"Do you know these people?" Clint asked.

"The Flynt brothers," Farrell said. "Dave and Robert."

"And the woman?"

"Robert's wife, Wendy."

"Do you have any idea why they'd try to do this?" Clint asked.

"No," Farrell said, "except to say that it was probably Wendy's play. These boys always did what she told them to do."

"That was the way it sounded to me," Clint said. "Like she was giving the orders."

"Still," Farrell said, "I'd wager somebody else put them up to it."

"We were followed here," Clint said. "Somebody's pulling the strings."

"Then I assume you'll be followed back," Farrell said. "Maybe you should do somethin' about that."

"Maybe I should."

The door opened and six men entered.

"Remove these bodies, take them to the undertaker," Farrell said.

"Yes, sheriff."

"Do you need anything further from me?" Clint asked.

"Yes," Sheriff Farrell said. "I need you not to kill anyone else between now, and tomorrow mornin' when you leave."

"I'll promise to do my best," Clint said. "Is that enough for you?"

"I suppose it'll have to be."

Clint nodded, and left the room.

***

When Randall opened the door to his room and let Clint in, Libbie looked up at him from her position on the bed. She had a glass of whiskey in her hand.

Clint looked at Randall, who shrugged and said, "I had a bottle in my saddlebag."

"I see."

"Drink?"

"No, thanks."

"Do you mind if I do?" the younger man asked.

"Go ahead."

Randall poured himself a drink and then stood off to one side.

"How did it go with the sheriff?" Libbie asked.

"Fine," Clint said. "He's letting us leave in the morning. Oh, he'd like me not to kill anyone else between now and then."

"Did he know those people?"

"Yes, a family here in town. He doesn't know why they'd do what they did, unless they were put up to it."

"So there's still someone out there," she said.

"Yes."

"Maybe whoever followed us here."

"Also correct."

"So what do we do?" she asked.

"Tomorrow," he said, "we find out who that is."

Chapter Thirty-Two

After a quick breakfast the next morning, the three of them walked to the livery.

"Are we being watched?" Libbie asked.

"No doubt," Clint said, "but it's only because word's gone around that I killed somebody yesterday."

"So they're staring at the Gunsmith," Randall said.

"Exactly."

"You must get that a lot," Randall said.

"My fair share."

"That used to happen to George, as well," Libbie commented.

Clint bit his lip. He didn't like being compared to Custer, who drew stares because he looked like such a dandy with his long, flowing blonde hair and mustache.

When they got to the livery, Clint saddled Eclipse while the hostler saddled the other two for Randall and Libbie. They then walked their mounts outside to find the sheriff standing there, waiting for them.

"Good-morning, Sheriff," Clint said. Can we do something for you?"

"You already are," Farrell said. "I just wanted to make sure you're leavin'."

"You know," Libbie said, "what happened was not our fault, Sheriff."

"That might be true, Ma'am," the lawman said, "but the fact is, you both attract trouble, and I really don't need that here. We're tryin' to build Hempstead up into a nice, family friendly town."

"Yeah," Clint said, "the Flynt family was real friendly, last night."

"Those were a coupla dumb boys being led around by the nose by a woman," Farrell said. "No loss, but still, I can't have you killin' anybody else."

"We get it, Sheriff," Clint said. "We're on our way."

"Ma'am," Farrell said, touching the brim of his hat before turning and walking away.

They all mounted up.

"How can we find out who's following us when everyone is watching us?" Randall asked.

"One of two things might happen," Clint said. "This time when we get out on the trail, I'll double back and find out who it is."

"And second?" Randall asked.

"This time nobody will follow us."

"Why not?" Libbie asked.

"Because we're heading back to Austin," Clint said, "and they know it."

***

When they got clear of town, Clint doubled back and returned within fifteen minutes.

"Anything?" Randall asked.

"It's like I suspected," Clint said. "Since we're heading back to Austin, there's no reason to trail us."

"Damn," Libbie said. "I'd really like to know who dislikes me this much."

"I'm sure it's not you, Libbie," Clint said.

"You think everyone disliked George the way you did?" she demanded.

"How I feel has nothing to do with it."

She glared at him, and Randall stepped in before either could speak again.

"We better keep going," he said. "How do we know the Flynt family doesn't have more members?"

"He's right," Clint said. "It may be that no one is following us. But that doesn't mean somebody else won't be coming for revenge."

They stopped talking and started riding.

***

They camped the first night and ate largely in silence.

"Would you gentlemen like me to take a watch?" Libbie asked them.

"No," Clint said. "You get some sleep. We'll handle that part."

"Good-night, then."

She went to her bedroll and covered herself up, her back to them.

"I'll take the first," Randall said.

"I'm going to check the horses before I turn in," Clint said. "Keep the fire, and the coffee pot, going."

"Right."

After making sure the horses were secured and cared for, Clint went to his own bedroll. But sleep was elusive, and he ended up getting to his feet after only an hour.

"Tired?" he asked, joining Randall at the fire.

"Exhausted."

"Turn in, then," Clint said. "I'm not going to sleep tonight."

Randall got to his feet.

"Because of what happened today?"

"No," Clint said, "I'm concerned with what's going to happen."

***

When they reached Austin they went back to the same hotel, reclaimed their rooms.

"Get some rest," Clint told Libbie.

"When can we leave?" she asked.

"Tomorrow, if you insist," Clint said.

"As soon as possible," she said. She looked at Randall. "Will you send Mr. McMay a telegram?"

"Saying what?" Randall asked.

"That we're on our way to Kansas," she said.

"Yes, Ma'am."

"Then I'll see you gentlemen later, for supper," she said. "I'm going to have a much needed bath."

She went to her room, leaving them in the lobby.

"Drink?" Clint asked.

"I thought you'd never ask."

They went to the hotel bar and ordered two beers.

"Do you think it's over here?" Randall asked.

"With three dead, I hope so," Clint said. "I don't really understand what those people wanted."

Chapter Thirty-Three

"I think she should go home," Randall said.

"Why?" Clint asked.

"As long as she's out here, doing her research, it seems her life is at risk."

"I assume she knows that," Clint said.

"So it's that important to her to get the story out?" Randall asked. "A story only some people will believe? That her husband was a hero?"

"More important than her own life?" Clint asked. "Definitely."

"Well," Randall said, "I'm afraid I just don't understand?"

"That's because you're a man," Clint said, "and a young one, at that."

"With a lot to learn," Randall said. "Yes, I've heard that from Mr. McMay, but he's always saying I have a lot to learn about publishing."

"I'm saying you have a lot to learn about people," Clint said, "and about women, in particular."

"You're probably right," Randall said, standing up.

"Where are you off to?" Clint asked.

"I'm going to send that telegram to Mr. McMay," Randall said. "I'll see you back here later."

As Randall left, Clint looked over and saw Virginia Gray sitting at the *Austin Journal's* table. He picked up his beer and walked over.

"You mind if I join you?" he asked.

"Not at all."

He sat across from her, noticed that she was also drinking beer.

"Did you get your story out?" he asked.

"It's written, but not out, yet."

"What's the problem?"

"The problem is I'm not the editor," she said. "It's up to him what goes in the paper, and when. I think he's waiting for something to happen."

"If that's the case," he said, "you should have been in Hempstead."

"Why?" She suddenly looked interested. "What happened there?"

"If I tell you, you'll have an exclusive—unless Hempstead has their own newspaper."

"They don't."

"Then you didn't hear this from me . . ." he said, and went on to tell her about the Flynt family . . .

***

Virginia Gray scribbled notes on a slip of paper she took from her drawstring purse.

"Did you get it all?" he asked.

"I believe so," she said, "but . . . you don't want your name attributed to this?"

"You can say what happened," Clint said, "say what I did, but not that you heard it from me."

Clint just wanted whoever had been behind sending the Flynt family after Libbie to read about what happened. Maybe it would put them off trying something like that again.

"Well, all right," she said, "but you've got to let me buy you another beer."

"That we can do," Clint said.

Virginia waved at the bartender, who came running over. The man smiled, obviously smitten with the lady journalist.

"Two more beers, Bill."

"Yes, Ma'am," the bartender said, "comin' up."

She folded her notes—wadded them up, actually— and stuffed them into her purse.

"So how much longer do you plan to be in town?" Virginia asked him as the bartender set down their fresh beers.

"We're probably leaving tomorrow," Clint said. "Mrs. Custer has had enough of Texas, I think."

"So where to next?"

"Not sure," Clint lied. No use telling the newspaper-woman where they would be next. He had already told her all he wanted to.

"Well, that's disappointing," she commented.

"What," he asked, "that I can't tell you where we'll be next?"

"No," she said, "that you're leaving town so soon. I thought we might get a chance to . . ."

"To what?" he asked. "Get to know each other?"

"Yes," she said, "but not the way you mean it."

"Really?" he asked. "And how do you mean it?"

"Well," she said, running her forefinger around the rim of her beer mug, "if you take me up to your room, I can show you how I mean it."

He studied her for a moment, wondering if she was speaking as a journalist, or as a woman. The look in her eyes quickly gave him his answer.

"Do you want to finish your beer first?" he asked.

"Not really," she said.

"Well then . . ." he said, standing.

Chapter Thirty-Four

When they got to Clint's room, no sooner had he locked the door than Virginia was on him. She kissed him while keeping her hands busy on his clothes. He pretty much had to drag her to the bed post with him so he could hang his gunbelt there. Once that was done he was able to get into the action with her.

He unbuttoned the jacket of her suit and peeled it off, then worked on the blouse. When he had that off, he saw that the severe cut of the jacket had been hiding a sleek body.

Her skirt came next, and then her frilly underthings. When she was naked, he got on his knees to kiss her belly, holding one of her smooth butt cheeks in each hand.

He moved his head lower and began to probe through the tangle of pubic hair with his tongue, finding her wet and waiting. She gasped and reached down to hold his head in her hands.

His shirt and boots were gone, but he still had his trousers on, and the smell and taste of her had so swollen his penis that it was painful.

He stood up and she helped him with his belt and buttons, tugged the trousers and underwear down to his ankles, so he could kick them away.

She took his hard cock in her hands, stroked it, caressed it, held it to her cheeks, rubbed it over her face, then finally opened her mouth and slid her lips over it. She did it gently at first, just taking the head in and wetting it, but then started taking more and more of it until she had the entire length in her mouth. She began to bob her head back and forth, then, sucked him wetly.

Abruptly, she pushed him until the back of his legs hit the bed, and he went onto his back. She crawled up onto the bed with him, got astride him and slid his hard penis into her wet pussy. She had small breasts with very large nipples, and they fascinated him as she began to ride him up and down. Finally, he decided to do more than just stare. He ran his hands up her body until he could cup each breast, enjoying the way her nipples felt against his palms. They were a pale color, almost blending in with her skin, but they hardened as he touched them and, somehow, got darker.

She began to rise and fall on him faster and faster, her breath coming in rasps—or was that him? No, it was both of them. He was moving his hips, trying to keep up with her, and they were both panting for breath. The air in the room became thick with the scent of their lovemaking—

her wetness, their perspiration, whatever smells their day had left affixed to their bodies. It all combined into an odor that inflamed their ardor.

She changed her position without breaking contact. Instead of sitting astride him, she leaned over and stretched out on him. Now those small breasts dangled in his face, and he reached for the nipples with his mouth and tongue. They continued moving their hips in unison, faster and faster, until he couldn't hold back any longer . . .

***

"Well," she said, lying on her back beside him, "it's nice to see that some reputations are well earned."

"Don't write about this," he said.

"Oh, don't worry," she said, "I won't. This is just between you and me."

"Good."

"What about you and Mrs. Custer?" she asked.

"What about us?"

"Are you . . . close?"

"No."

"Not in any way?"

"Sure as hell not this way," he said, putting his hand on her bare thigh.

"Then were you and he friends?" she asked. "You and General Custer?"

"Not ever," Clint said. "We despised each other."

"Why?"

"Because we were different men," Clint said, "and we knew it. He wanted to strut and have people ooh and ahh. I wanted people to leave me alone, even look away when I passed."

"Then why did you become the Gunsmith?"

He turned his head and looked at her.

"I'm not trying to interview you," she said. "I'd really like to know."

"Becoming the Gunsmith was never a deliberate thing," he said. "I didn't decide to become the Gunsmith, I just . . . did."

"Could you have avoided it?"

"Possibly," Clint said, "but I don't think I was smart enough to realize what was happening. And by the time I did, it was too late to do anything about it. Anything, that is, but live with it."

"Interesting," she said. "Do you get to make any decisions about your life?"

"Day to day," he said, "like the decision to come up here with you." He squeezed her thigh. "That's one I'll never regret."

She smiled, rolled into his arms, and kissed him.

Chapter Thirty-Five

When Clint came back down to the lobby Randall was there. Virginia Gray had already left the hotel.

"Did you get your telegram sent?" Clint asked.

"Yes. What have you been up to?"

"Just waiting," Clint said.

"Are we committed to leaving tomorrow?" Randall asked.

"I believe so."

"Then all that's left to do here is have a good meal, and get a good night's sleep."

"I suppose so," Clint said. "Shall we go up and get the lady?"

"By all means," Randall said.

As they crossed the lobby to the stairs Clint asked, "Did you receive a reply to your message?"

"I did," Randall said. "All it said was 'good work'."

"I suppose he's just glad we're leaving here," Clint said. "Safely."

"I suppose you're right."

***

They collected a freshly scrubbed Libbie Custer from her room, and all went to supper.

"We'll stay in the hotel," Clint said.

"Why?" Libbie asked.

"There's no point in having you walk around out there with a target on your back."

"He's right," Randall said. "Staying inside is safer."

"But, if they tried once, won't they try again?" Libbie asked.

"We don't know," Clint said. "Those three may have been the only ones."

"What about whoever was following us?"

"It might have been one of them," Clint said. "Who knows?"

"Don't you want to know?" Libbie asked.

"I'd rather we just catch the train tomorrow and get out of here," Clint aid, "with you safe."

So they ate in the hotel dining room, which at that time of the evening—after supper—was half empty.

"Nobody seems to be paying any special attention to us," Randall said.

"That could be a good thing," Clint said, "or a bad thing. In this instance, I think it's good."

"Are we supposed to hide in our rooms all night?" Libbie asked.

"That's exactly what you're going to do," Clint said. "Stay in your room. Don't come out until we get you in the morning, at which time we'll board the train."

"Whatever you say."

"You want to continue, right?" Clint asked.

"Of course I do," she said. "A Custer doesn't quit."

Clint bit his tongue.

***

They walked Libbie back to her room.

"Lock the door," Clint said, "and don't open it unless it's one of us."

"Maybe," she said, "Mr. Randall could come by later, and we could . . . talk?"

Randall looked at Clint, who simply shrugged.

"I could do that, Ma'am," he said. "Keep you company for a little while."

"Thank you, Lucius."

She closed the door, leaving them in the hall.

As they walked to their own rooms Randall said, "You told me I needed to learn about women."

"I did."

"Was she asking me for . . . something more than just . . . company?"

"Like what? Oh, I see."

"I mean," Randall said, "she's a handsome woman, but I'm not—"

"Stop right there," Clint said. "I don't think that was what she had in mind."

"Oh?"

"She still loves her husband, Lucius," Clint said. "I'm sure she just wants to talk, to pass the time."

They stopped in front of their doors.

"Pass the time with me?" he asked. "Why not you?"

"I think you know the answer to that," Clint said. "She and I could never spend any time together alone. We'd end up . . . arguing about Custer."

"But I didn't know him," Randall said. "What can I talk about?"

"She doesn't want you to talk, Lucius," Clint said, "she just wants you to listen."

Randall turned and looked back toward Libbie's door.

"When should I go back?"

"Give it a couple of hours," Clint said, "then go and knock on her door. From that point on, she'll do all the talking. Of that I'm sure."

Randall nodded, and went into his room. Clint waited a moment, then entered his own.

Chapter Thirty-Six

On the train the next day, they made sure that all three horses were secure in the stock car before getting themselves settled.

"Isn't the passenger car up there?" Libbie asked.

"It is," Clint said, "but I got you a sleeping cabin, even though the trip is not as long, this time."

"Why?"

"To keep you away from the other passengers," Clint said. "And we'll be bringing you your food, as to make sure you don't get another glass sandwich."

"And you and Lucius?"

"We'll be in the passenger car," Clint said. "I may be using Mr. McMay's money, but I'll only stretch it so far."

He opened the door for her and allowed her to enter, then set her bags down on the floor.

"Your trunk is in the baggage car."

When they went from Austin to Hempstead, they left her trunk in the hotel.

"I'm surprised you haven't managed to lose it by now," she said to Clint.

"To tell you the truth," he said, "so am I."

***

In the passenger car, Clint and Randall sat side-by-side, directly across from a drummer who had a sample case almost as large as Libbie's trunk.

"Do you think she's safe in there, alone?" Randall asked.

"The door's locked, the lock is strong, and she won't open it for anyone but us. She's safe enough."

"Why did you want us in the passenger car?" Randall asked.

"To see if anyone's interested in us," Clint said. "Or in me."

"I see."

"How did it go last night?" Clint asked. "Keeping her company in her room."

"You were right," he said. "She just wanted to talk. A lot of it was about what's going into the second book. By saying it out loud, I think she locked it in her mind until she can sit down and write it."

"And she never tried to get your pants off?" Clint asked.

"No!" Randall said. "You were right. But . . ."

"But what?"

"I was sort of nervous when I walked in," Randall said. "And, thinking about it, I got . . . excited."

"But it didn't happen."

"No, it didn't."

"Then maybe you should have gone out and got yourself a woman, after," Clint said.

Randall turned his head and stared at him.

"I didn't think of that."

"See?" Clint said. "You've got a lot to learn."

***

They went to the dining car, ate their supper, then ordered something for Libbie and took it to her cabin.

"Who is it?" she asked, after they knocked.

"It's us," Clint said. "We brought you something to eat."

She opened the door and Clint handed her the tray he'd been holding. On it was a steaming bowl, and a large piece of crusty bread, and a cup of coffee.

"What is it?" she asked.

"Beef stew."

"Did you check it for glass?"

"Yes."

She stared at him.

"I was kidding," she said.

"I'm not."

"Well, thank you for this," she said.

"We'll pick up the tray later," Clint said. "And Randall can come and keep you company, if you like."

"Lucius did it last night," Libbie said. "Why don't you do it tonight."

"Me?"

"Sure," she said. "Take turns, like you do when you keep watch on the trail."

"Oh, well, okay."

"Thank you again."

She backed up and he pulled the door closed.

***

"What do you think is on her mind?" Randall asked when they sat back down.

"Hmm?"

"Why does she want you to come and keep her company?"

"I don't know."

"Maybe," Randall said, "she has something in mind for you that she didn't have for me?"

"I doubt that," Clint said.

"Why?"

"I'm not her type," Clint said. "I'm neither a dandy, or blonde."

Chapter Thirty-Seven

Later, Clint left Randall in the passenger car and went to the sleeping car. He knocked on Libbie's door.

"Mr. Adams," she said, as she opened it.

"I'm here to collect your tray," he said.

"I thought perhaps you were here to pass the time."

"Oh, that's right," he said. "You asked me . . ."

". . . yes, I did . . ."

". . . to do that, didn't you?"

"Yes. Can you stay a while?"

"Well, sure," he said.

He stepped inside and closed the door behind him. The cabin was small, with only the small bed to sit on.

"Have a seat," she said. "I can't offer you anything."

"I should have brought coffee. Sorry."

"It's okay."

He sat on one end of the bed, and she on the other.

"What have you and Lucius been doing?" she asked.

"Looking out the window," Clint said.

"Ah," she said, "I've been doing quite a lot of that myself."

He nodded, trying to think of something he could say that they wouldn't argue about, now that they'd talked about looking out the window.

"So, where are we going when we get to Kansas?" Clint asked.

"We'll start at Fort Riley," she said. "When George was attached to the Seventh Calvary as a Lieutenant Colonel, we started there. Afterward he went on to Fort Wallace, Fort Hays, Fort Dodge, Fort Larned and some others, while I remained in Fort Riley."

Clint seemed to remember that Custer was court martialed for marching his men from Fort Wallace to Fort Hays without orders. He was found guilty and forced to stand down for a year. He wondered if Libbie was going to bother writing about that?

"Do you remember anything about George in Kansas?" she asked.

Okay, now she was testing him.

"No," he lied, "not very much."

She went on to talk about George pursuing Indians throughout Kansas, Oklahoma and Nebraska. Clint continued to bite his tongue, as he had been doing for many days, now, while Libbie praised her husband's good points and completely ignored the bad.

"What are you thinking?" she asked.

Startled, he looked at her. Had she been reading his mind?

"I was, uh, wondering if it was a lonely time for you, what with him out chasing Indians all the time."

"There were other officers' wives there," she said, "but in fact it was rather lonely. The other officers didn't like George because he was so brilliant, which seemed to extend to the way their wives felt about me."

"That's a shame."

They were silent for a while, and then she suddenly exploded.

"Oh, I don't know why we're doing this!"

"What?"

"Trying to talk," she said. "You and I have nothing in common. You hated George."

"He hated me," Clint said, "so we were even."

"At least when I talk to Lucius I don't get the feeling he's having all these horrible thoughts of his own."

"Look, Libbie," Clint said, "I'm here to keep you safe, not to sing your husband's praises with you."

"That much is painfully obvious," she said. "Why don't you just take the tray and go."

"I'll do that," he said. "I'll see you in the morning when we bring you your breakfast."

"Fine," she said, turning her head to stare out the window as he left.

In the hall he took a deep breath and headed back with the tray.

***

Later, he and Randall were sitting in the dining car with a beer each, staring out the window at the darkness.

"You didn't tell me what happened with Mrs. Custer," Randall said.

"Just what I thought would happen," Clint said. "She sang her husband's praises until she could see I wasn't buying it."

"What do you know about their time in Kansas?" the younger man asked.

"Custer was court martialed at one point," Clint said. "They stood him down for a year, but Phil Sheridan brought him back early to lead the campaign against the Cheyenne."

"*General* Sheridan?"

"That's right."

"And what was Custer's rank at that time?"

"Lieutenant Colonel."

"And did it go well?"

"Did it ever go well for Custer?" Clint asked.

"I always thought he was considered a brilliant tactician."

"By some, maybe," Clint said, turning his head to stare out at the darkness, "not by me."

Chapter Thirty-Eight

The town of Fort Riley was behind the fort, which was inhabited by the Tenth Cavalry when Clint, Randall and Libbie Custer rode in.

Once again, they took care of their horses before getting a hotel room, which was an easy thing to do. Fort Riley was not a bustling town.

"This town was much lovelier when we were here with the Seventh," Libbie commented.

"Well, being in town was safer than out on the plains while the Indians were raiding," Clint pointed out. "Not much of that going on now."

"Where did you and the Colonel stay?" Randall asked Libbie.

"In the fort," she said. "There was an officer's quarters for the single men, and then each married officer received their own quarters."

In the lobby Clint said to Libbie, "Why don't you go to your room and freshen up. Lucius and I will meet you down here in half an hour."

"Half an hour to freshen up?" she said. "Thanks."

"Fine," Clint said, "take an hour."

She waved her hand and went up. Obviously she was still miffed that this time Clint had managed to leave her trunk in the train station in Kansas City.

"Okay," Randall said, when Libbie was gone, "so tell me, were we followed here?"

"I didn't hear anything, or feel anything," Clint admitted, accepting his key from the clerk. "So I don't think so."

"Sir?" the clerk said.

"Yes?"

"Um, Mrs. Custer," the middle-aged man said, "is that . . . was she married to General Custer?"

"That's right."

"My, my . . ." he said.

As Clint and Randall went up the stairs with their saddlebags, Randall asked, "How many ranks did Custer have? I've heard him called Colonel, General—"

"Lieutenant Colonel when he was here," Clint said. "His attitude often got him promoted, court martialed, busted, and promoted again."

"Quite a career," Randall said.

"You can say that again," Clint said. "and not one that a lot of other officers would've wanted—especially the way it ended."

***

Clint was freshening up with the pitcher-and-basin when there was a knock at the door. He grabbed his gun and, bare chested, went to the door.

"Who is it?"

"Sheriff Corbett," a man's voice said. "I'd like to talk to you, Mr. Adams."

Clint opened the door a crack, saw a grey-haired, mustachioed man, with a badge on his chest, standing there.

"I'm alone," the lawman said. "You are Clint Adams, the Gunsmith, right?"

"That's right."

"You mind if I come in?"

"Come ahead," Clint said, opening the door wide and stepping back.

"Sorry to bother you," Corbett said, closing the door behind him.

"You mind if I keep washing?"

"Not at all."

Clint put the gun down on the dresser, right next to the basin.

"Word travels fast, huh?" he asked.

"What? Oh, you mean my knowing you were here? Yes, I keep close tabs on who comes into town. I heard about you and Mrs. Custer, and figured I might as well not waste any time."

Clint turned to the lawman, drying his hands and arms with a white towel, his gun still within easy reach.

"What's on your mind, Sheriff?"

"Just wondering, is all," Corbett said. "What brings you and the lady to Fort Riley?"

"The lady has written a book about her husband," Clint said, "and is planning another one. Since she was stationed here with her husband back in sixty-six, sixty-seven, she wanted to come by and have a look."

"A lot changes in twenty years."

"That's true," Clint said. "The Tenth Cavalry is here instead of the Seventh."

"And there are no Indians for them to battle," Corbett pointed out. "When she was here with her husband—"

"Were you here then, Sheriff?" Clint asked.

"No," the lawman said, "I came along later. But I heard stories—"

"About what?"

"Custer, of course," he said. "And I've heard stories about you, as well."

You can't believe what you've heard about either of us," Clint said.

"That's why I'm here, then," Corbett said. "To find out the real story."

Clint pulled on his shirt and said, "Buy me a beer and maybe I'll tell you."

Chapter Thirty-Nine

The sheriff took Clint to a saloon across the street called the Panhandle Saloon.

"Why that name?" Clint asked, as they walked in. "We're nowhere near the panhandle."

"The owner is from there," Corbett said.

"He's a Texan?"

"No," the sheriff said, laughing, "he's from the Florida panhandle."

"I didn't know Florida had a panhandle," Clint said. "I mean, I've been to Florida, but—"

"It's where Pensacola is," the lawman said, "and Panama City."

Clint had not ever been to either of those places.

They went inside, found a saloon that was only half full.

"Does it get crowded later?" Clint asked.

"This is about it," Corbett said, "except when the soldiers come from the fort. This is not exactly what you'd call a thriving community. If it wasn't for the fort, this town would be dead."

"That's a shame."

"Take that back table," Corbett said. "I'll bring the beers."

Clint sat as Corbett went to the bar. He returned carrying four beer mugs.

"I didn't know how long this story would be," he explained, sitting opposite Clint.

"Well, that all depends," Clint said, picking up a beer mug.

"On what?" Corbett asked.

"On how much you want to know, and why you want to know it," Clint explained.

"I'm not looking for your history," the sheriff said. "I'm just askin' why you're here, and what I might have to deal with."

"All right, then," Clint said, and proceeded to tell the lawman what Libbie was doing, what he was doing, and what they had experienced, so far.

"Jesus," Corbett said, when Clint was done. He had moved on to his second beer. "Kidnappers? Why would anyone care what the woman writes about her husband?"

"Exactly," Clint said. "But somebody does."

"Who?"

Clint finished his first beer, grabbed his second,

"Who, indeed?" he asked.

***

The sheriff was satisfied that Clint wasn't looking for trouble, but would do what he had to do to keep Libbie Custer safe.

When they left the Panhandle Saloon they stopped a moment.

"If there's any trouble," the lawman said, "let me know."

"Somehow," Clint said, "I have the feeling you'll already know."

Sheriff Corbett went to make his rounds; Clint went back to his hotel.

***

Sitting in his room he thought about what he and the sheriff had discussed. Who stood to benefit from kidnapping Libbie Custer, from doing her any harm? Was someone trying to keep her from writing another book? Or was the goal something else, entirely?

He left his room, crossed the hall and knocked on Randall's door.

"Do you still have any whiskey?" he asked, when the man opened the door.

"Some," Randall said. "Come in."

Clint sat in a chair in the corner while Randall retrieved the bottle from his saddlebag. He found two glasses, poured, and handed one to Clint. Then he sat on the bed.

"Ready for supper?" Randall asked.

"Soon," Clint said. "I just had a couple of beers with the local law."

"Did you seek him out?"

"No, he came to my room. He heard we were here and wanted to know why."

"What did you tell him?"

"Everything."

"All of it?"

"Yes," Clint said.

"What did he say?"

"He brought up a question," Clint said, "a question I should have thought of. And now I want to put that question to you."

"All right," Randall said. "Hopefully I can answer it."

"Who would benefit from kidnapping Libbie Custer?" Clint asked.

"That's the question?"

"That's it."

"What makes you think I'll know the answer?"

"Because I think I know the answer," Clint said.

Chapter Forty

"If you know the answer," Randall asked, "why are you asking me?"

"I want to see if you come up with the same one."

"Why?"

"Because you're a smart young man."

Randall frowned, sipped his drink, poured another.

"Okay, ask me again."

"If Libbie had been kidnapped, who would have benefited from it?"

"Well, assuming she was taken for a ransom, then whoever the kidnappers were, they would have benefited."

"Okay," Clint said, "the Flynt family were the actual kidnappers. But who would have put them up to it?"

"Somebody who knew where we were," Randall said.

"Uh-huh."

"Wait," Randall said, "are you suggesting—do you think Libbie did it herself? To get attention for her books?"

"I don't think she had anything to do with it," Clint said.

"Why not? Remember, she killed that woman. Maybe she did it to keep her quiet."

"She was angry," Clint said, "and then she was shocked. I don't think she's that good an actress."

"So who else do you think—wait a minute. No."

Randall got up, walked to his window and looked out, then looked back at Clint.

"You think Mr. McMay sent those three to kidnap Mrs. Custer?"

"It's possible," Clint said. "A kidnapping like that would get into a lot of newspapers. Wouldn't that sell plenty of books?"

"Well, yes, but . . . they got killed."

"I don't think McMay planned on that," Clint said, "but he took that chance by getting me involved, didn't he?"

"If he did it."

"What do you think, Lucius?" Clint asked. "Would he?"

Randall walked to the bed and sat down.

"I know him really well," the younger man said. "He knew my family—"

"He told me that," Clint said. "He also told me to make sure you didn't get hurt."

"Why would he think I would get hurt?"

"Either because you were going to the Wild West," Clint said, "or because he had planned the kidnapping, and didn't want you to get involved."

"Oh my god," Randall said. "You might be right. Henry does whatever he can to promote a book."

"I thought he might," Clint said. "After all, he's using me, isn't he?"

Randall looked away.

"Lucius?"

"He told me that he was going to feed the newspapers stories of the Gunsmith accompanying Mrs. George Armstrong Custer on her research trip."

"And then the kidnap story, as well."

"Shit," Randall said. "I'm not happy about this, Clint. Believe me."

"I'm not either." He put his glass down, having not touched the whiskey.

"What are you going to do?" Randall asked.

"We'll finish up here," Clint said, "and then take Libbie back . . . where? To San Francisco?"

"No," Randall said, "the publishing company is based in Chicago and New York. Henry wants me to bring Libbie to the Chicago office."

"That's fine with me."

"Will you come to Chicago to confront him?"

"No," Clint said. "I'll figure out how to do that another way."

"And what about Libbie?" Randall asked. "If you're sure she wasn't in on it, will you tell her about it?"

"I don't think so," Clint said, "but I'll decide that later, too."

"If you tell her, she might not let Henry publish the second book."

"Or," Clint said, "she'll be impressed with what he did to publicize the first one."

Randall's eyes went wide.

"You think she'd be impressed?"

Clint stood up, headed for the door.

"Why not?" he asked. "She was impressed by Custer."

"Where are you going?"

"I'm going to change my clothes for supper," Clint said. "Can you be ready in fifteen minutes?"

"Sure."

Clint opened the door to leave.

"Wait!" Randall said.

Clint turned.

"Does this mean we don't have to be careful anymore?" Randall asked. "I mean, we can walk down the street with her?"

"I don't know," Clint said, "but I intend to find out."

Chapter Forty-One

During supper at a restaurant they found down the street, Clint could see that Lucius Randall was having trouble with what they now knew, or at least, suspected.

Libbie noticed.

"What's going on, Lucius?"

"Ma'am?"

"You look like you've got something on your mind," she said.

His eyes went wide and he looked at Clint.

She looked at Clint.

"All right, you tell me," she said.

"Oh, he just got a telegram from McMay telling him to bring you to Chicago when this trip is over."

She looked at Randall again, who had found something very interesting on his plate.

"That's no surprise," she said. "That was the plan."

"Well," Clint said, "maybe Lucius didn't know the plan ahead of time."

"I thought Henry kept you apprised of everything, Lucius," she said.

"Um," he said, without looking up, "apparently not everything."

Libbie sat back, looked at her chicken, then dropped her utensils onto her plate with a metallic bang.

"Okay, what's going on?" she demanded.

Clint gave Randall a stern look, then glanced at Libbie.

"Lucius and I had a discussion this morning about the kidnap attempt on you," Clint said.

"What about it?"

"We were wondering who would have benefited from it."

"Well, the kidnappers, naturally."

"No," Clint said, "somebody put them up to it."

She frowned.

"Why would someone do that?"

"For publicity," Clint said. "It would make your books sell better."

Her eyes went wide.

"Do you think that I—"

"No!" Clint said, cutting her short. "Not you."

"Then who—oh, wait. You mean . . . Henry?"

"That's my thought."

"So . . . you're saying the kidnapping wasn't real. But . . . but those people, they died."

"Not part of the plan, I'm sure," Clint said.

"But when you broke into the room, they went for their guns," she said. "They made it happen."

"Spur of the moment," Clint said. "It was like a reflex."

"And it got them killed," she said. "If you're right."

"Yes," Clint said, "if I'm right."

"So how do we find out?" she asked.

"We ask him."

"In Chicago?"

"Oh, I'm not going to Chicago," Clint said. "I think Lucius should send McMay a telegram telling him to come to Kansas City. Then we can talk to him, and if you still want to work with him, he can escort you back to Chicago."

"I just need a couple of days here," Libbie said.

"I can send the telegram tonight, and see when he can meet us," Randall said.

"Tell him two days," Clint said.

"And what if we're not in Kansas City, by then?" Randall asked.

"Then he can wait for us," Clint said.

"I can't believe this," Libbie said. "At the time it seemed so real."

"Let's remember," Clint said, "it might have been. This is just a theory of mine."

"Well," Libbie said, "it makes sense. They could only have planned a kidnapping if they knew we were coming.

And the only one who knew we were there, was Henry. Damn it, no this makes more and more sense."

"What will you do if it does turn out that Mr. McMay was behind it?" Randall asked.

She picked up her fork and addressed her plate of food again.

"I'm not sure, Lucius," she said. "I'll just have to think about it."

***

They strolled back to the hotel, darkness falling on Fort Riley.

"It feels to me like nobody's paying special attention to us," Libbie said. "Is that my imagination?"

"No," Clint said, "it's not. We may be in the clear, here."

"But the sheriff heard you're here," Randall reminded him. "Doesn't that mean others will, too?"

"Probably," Clint said. "We'll just have to wait and see what happens."

"In the morning I'd like to take a walk through the fort," Libbie said. "Do you think we can arrange that?"

"We'll give it a try," Clint said, "and see what the C.O. has to say about it."

"Then goodnight, boys," Libbie said, in the lobby. "See you for breakfast."

"Drink?" Clint asked Randall.

"I don't think so," Randall said. "I'm just going to go to my room. I'll see you in the morning."

"Okay, Lucius," Clint said. "See you then."

***

When Lucius Randall came out of the hotel a half an hour later, Clint fell in behind and followed him.

Chapter Forty-Two

At breakfast the next morning, Clint didn't say anything about following Randall the night before. And Randall, himself, was very quiet.

"You boys don't have very much to say," Libbie observed.

"I'm just tired," Randall said.

"I'm saving myself for the C.O.," Clint said.

"I think I'll be able to handle him, Clint," Libbie said. "Will you let me try?"

"Hey," Clint said, "it's your show."

They settled their bill and walked over to the fort to the commanding officer's office. They had to get past his aide, Lieutenant Bennett Wayne, first. The young man let them into his outer office and regarded them from behind his desk.

"Lieutenant Wayne," Libbie said, "my name is Elizabeth Bacon Custer. My husband was George Armstrong Custer."

"Yes, Ma'am."

"Do you know who he was?"

"Yes, Ma'am, I'm familiar with Colonel Custer."

"My husband and I were stationed here for a short time," Libbie said, "and I'd like to take a walk around the fort."

"Well, Ma'am, we really don't allow civilians to do that—"

"Lieutenant," Clint said, "could we see your C.O. so Mrs. Custer could put her request to him, personally?"

"Sir . . . and you are?"

"This is Lucius Randall," Clint said, "he works for Mrs. Custer's book publisher, and my name is Clint Adams."

"Sir?" the Lieutenant said, his eyes widening.

"Clint Adams."

"The, uh, the Gunsmith, sir?"

"That's right," Libbie said, "he's the Gunsmith. Does that count more than me being the wife of a former decorated officer who died performing his duty?"

"Ma'am?"

"I said—"

"I heard you, Ma'am, but your husband died—"

"In the line of duty, Lieutenant," Clint said, cutting the man off before he could say something unfortunate. "Now, could you ask your Commanding Officer if he'll see us?"

"Yes, sir," the Lieutenant said. "I will ask him."

He turned, knocked on the C.O.'s door, and entered.

177

"Jesus Christ," Libbie said, "what else did George have to do—"

"Relax, Libbie," Clint said.

"He died for his country!" she snapped. "Why does it matter how or why?"

"Let's just wait and see what happens," Clint said.

"What'll happen is that they'll let us walk around the fort, but only because you're the Gunsmith."

"Why does that matter?" Randall asked. "As long as we get to do it?"

She glared at him and simply said, "You wouldn't understand."

The young Lieutenant came out of his C.O.'s office and left the door open.

"Colonel Lymington will see you now."

"Thank you," Libbie said, and marched in ahead of Clint and Randall.

Colonel Lymington was a tall, barrel-chested man in his fifties, with steel grey hair and mustache. He stood behind his desk and smiled as they entered.

"Mrs. Custer."

"Thank you for seeing us, Colonel," she said.

"Of course," Lymington said. "Your husband has a very large place in the history of this fort. Out of respect for him, I'm happy to meet with you."

He remained where he was, however, and she had to reach across the desk to shake his hand. In Clint's eyes, he was now showing as much respect as he was speaking about.

"And Mr. Adams? A pleasure, sir."

Clint stood back from the desk and nodded. If Lymington wanted to shake his hand he'd have to come out from behind the desk. He didn't.

"And sir?" the C.O. said to Randall.

"Lucius Randall, sir," Randall said, shaking the Colonel's hand. "I work for Mrs. Custer's publisher."

"Ah, so this is some sort of fact finding mission?" the Colonel asked. He kept switching his gaze back and forth between Clint and Libbie. "Please, have a seat."

There were two chairs, so Libbie took one and Clint the other.

"I would really just like to familiarize myself with the fort," Libbie said, "and see how it may have changed since George and I were here. It shouldn't take very long."

"I wouldn't think that should be a problem," the Colonel said. "Of course, I would have to assign an escort for you. We can't have civilians simply wandering around the post—even such eminent civilians as you."

"Of course," Libbie said. "I understand perfectly. But if I may, I'd ask that the escort not be your aide."

Lymington smiled.

"You'll have to forgive the Lieutenant," he said. "I'll have a talk with him about his manners toward visiting, uh, celebrities."

"I don't want to be treated as a celebrity," Libbie said. "Just as the wife of a former officer."

"Of course. I'll have Sergeant Troy show you around. He has enough years under his belt to display the proper respect."

"Thank you, Colonel," Libbie said. "I appreciate it."

"If you'll wait here I'll have my aide go and fetch the sergeant."

Lymington finally came out from behind his desk. The reason he hadn't done it before became evident. He had a stiff leg, probably from an injury earlier in his career.

He went to the door, opened it, stuck his head out and asked the Lieutenant to go and find Sergeant Troy and bring him back, immediately.

"It won't be long," Lymington said, limping back behind his desk and sitting.

"Is that a recent injury, Colonel?" Randall asked. "The leg, I mean."

Both Libbie and Clint knew enough not to ask, but Randall didn't have the same tact.

"Not recent, no," Lymington said. "A bullet during the war. It's getting worse as I get older."

"I'm sorry to hear that," Randall said.

For the rest of the time Lymington talked with Libbie about her first book—which he had not read—and the second, which she would soon start.

***

Sergeant Troy was a grizzled old veteran in his sixties, had probably been a sergeant since the Civil War, and was happy with the rank. When he arrived, the Colonel told him what his assignment was for the next few hours, "or however long it took."

"Simply take Mrs. Custer wherever she wants to go on the post."

"Yessir. And, uh, the gentlemen?"

"They will follow along, I'm sure."

"We'll try not to get in the way, Sergeant," Clint promised.

"Bring them back here when you're through, Sergeant," Lymington said

"Whatever you say, Colonel," Troy said, saluting. "Ma'am? If you'll come this way?"

"Thank you, Sergeant," she said, and then "thank you, Colonel," before she followed the sergeant out.

Chapter Forty-Three

Sgt. Troy did just as his commanding officer ordered him to do. He took Libbie anywhere she wanted to go on the post, including the quarters she shared with her husband when they were assigned there to the 7th Cavalry.

Clint and Randall followed along behind, but remained outside when Libbie went into the quarters to look them over. When she and Troy came out she was very quiet.

They looked at some of the other barracks and Libbie pretty much strolled through the entire fort in about three hours. Clint was able to catch the expression on Sgt. Troy's face from time-to-time when the man was standing behind Libbie. He was not happy at having been given this particular task. What Clint didn't know was if the Sgt. didn't like the idea of being a tour guide, or if it had something to do with the way he felt about Custer.

At one point, while Libbie was inside her old barracks with Troy, Clint decided to put Randall on the spot and see how the young man reacted.

"I saw you last night," he said.

"Yeah," Randall said, "and I saw you, too."

"No," Clint said, "I mean after that."

Randall gave Clint a sideways glance.

"You did?" he asked. "What was I doing?"

"It looked to me like you were sneaking around."

"Sneaking?" Randal asked. "I wasn't sneaking. I just went out for a walk—"

"I followed you, Lucius," Clint said.

"You—what?" Randall asked. "So, who does that make sneaky?"

"I was waiting outside and followed you when you came out. It occurred to me you might be working with McMay on this business of publicity, so I wanted to see if you actually would send him a telegram. You didn't. Actually, I didn't even know if you or Libbie would come out," Clint said. "I'm not totally sold on McMay being behind the kidnapping, but if he is, I figured he couldn't be doing it alone. That meant either you, or Libbie, was involved."

"So now you think it was me?"

At that moment Libbie and Troy came out.

"Why don't we talk about it later?" Clint said.

Randall remained quiet, and Clint knew the young man's mind would be racing until that moment.

***

When Libbie told Sgt. Troy she was done, Clint could see the relief on the man's heavily lined face. He brought them back to the C.O.'s office, and left them in the hands of the aide, Lieutenant Wayne.

As Troy turned to leave, he leaned into Clint and asked, "Does she really believe everythin' she's been sayin' about her husband?"

"Every word," Clint said.

"That poor woman," Sgt. Troy said, shaking his head as he left.

"The Colonel asked me to bring you in as soon as you got back," Lieutenant Wayne told them.

They all filed into the C.O.'s office.

"Mrs. Custer." This time the man limped out from behind the desk and shook all their hands. "How did it go? Did the sergeant do what I told him to do?"

"Your Sergeant was very helpful," Libbie said. "Thank you for loaning him to us."

"And did you get what you needed for your book?" he asked her.

"I did fine, Colonel," Libbie said.

"Will you be wanting to go to any of the other forts?" he asked. "I could send word ahead to them to let them know that you're coming, make sure they pay you the same courtesies you received here, today."

"I'll keep that in mind," Libbie said, "and let you know. Thank you."

He shook hands with each of them again, and they left his office.

"So, what about the other forts?" Clint asked, when they got outside. "Do you want to ride out to them?"

"I'm a little tired right now," Libbie said. "I think I'll make up my mind tomorrow. I'm still dealing with this whole phony kidnapping thing."

"Just remember what I said Libbie," Clint told her. "It's a theory that McMay's behind it. It could still be somebody else."

Randall looked away

"Who else is there but us three?" Libbie asked. "No, I think you're right. I'm just not quite sure what I'm going to do about it."

"Like you said, we can talk about it tomorrow," he told her "Since you're tired, do you want us to bring some food up to your room?"

"That would be great," she said. "Thank you."

"Let's get back to the hotel, then," Clint said.

Chapter Forty-Four

They took Libbie back to the hotel and waited in the lobby while she went upstairs.

"Clint—" Randall started.

"I'm going to get her some food," Clint said. "You go to your room and I'll come by later so we can talk about you sneaking out last night."

"I didn't sneak—"

"We'll talk about it," Clint said, cutting him off.

He waited while Randall went up the stairs to the second floor, then we went into the dining room.

***

He knocked on Libbie's door and she allowed him to enter with the tray he was carrying. Everything was covered by a cloth napkin, except for a tall glass of lemonade.

"That smells good," she said.

"I had them prepare you a chicken dinner," he said, setting the tray down. "I wasn't sure what you'd want to drink, but I remembered you had lemonade one night."

"That's fine," she said. "Will you be eating with Randall tonight?"

"I'm going to see him now in his room," Clint said, not answering the exact question she asked. The truth was, he wasn't sure what was going to happen with Randall . . .

***

. . . the night before, when Randall came out of the hotel, Clint followed the young man through the streets of Fort Riley until they came to a two-story building that wasn't a hotel, restaurant or saloon. It actually looked abandoned, but when Randall knocked, somebody opened the door. Light streamed out weakly, and let him in.

Clint crossed the street then to see what he could, but windows were covered from the inside, either deliberately, or just by an accumulation of dirt. And there was nothing on the door to indicate what the building might be.

He went back across the street to wait and when Randall came out fifteen minutes later, he followed him back to the hotel . . .

***

Now he left Libbie's room and walked down the hall to Randall's. When he had to knock twice, he knew he'd

187

made a mistake by not pursuing the issue with Randall sooner. He forced the door and entered, already knowing that Lucius Randall had lit out.

Clint immediately left the hotel and walked to the building he had followed Randall to the night before. In the fading daylight, it still looked completely abandoned. He pressed his shoulder to the front door, exerted more pressure, and popped it open. He left the door open behind him for some light, but it didn't matter. The place was completely empty. There were marks on the floor that made it look like it might have been a store at one time, with shelves and display cases. Even the walls had marks where items had hung. There was a back room, but that was also empty.

He saw an oil lamp on the floor and reached down to touch it. It was warm, as if it had just been blown out. He picked it up, lit a match and touched it to the wick. There was plenty of oil, and the lamp illuminated the room.

He walked around until he found a stairway to a second floor. He went up, the stairs creaking beneath his weight. When he got to the top, the lamp showed that the second floor was as empty as the first—except for one thing.

"Don't kill me," the man crouching in the corner said.

Chapter Forty-Five

"I'm not going to kill you," Clint said. "Stand up."

The man stood. He didn't look like a drunk or a hobo, his clothes were presentable and his hands and face were clean. In the light of the lamp he looked about thirty.

"What are you doing here?" Clint asked.

"I—I'm just—I was lookin' for a place to sleep," the man said.

"Or you're waiting for Lucius Randall to come back."

The man's eyes went wide.

"Did he send you here?"

"No," Clint said, "I followed him when he came last night. Why did you think he'd be coming back tonight?"

"I was just—"

"Hoping?"

The man nodded.

"Let me guess. He had a job for you and some of your friends, and this was your meeting place. He came last night and called it off."

"H-how did you know?"

"Because I'm the reason he called it off. Did he give you any details?"

"No," the man said, "he sent a telegram from Texas, saying he'd meet me here. And pay us a lot of money. But now . . ."

". . . he's not."

"No."

"What's your name?"

"Noah Lane."

"You and your friends, Noah, you do odd jobs?"

"That's right."

"Who put you and Lucius together?"

"I dunno. He never said."

"And if he would've asked you and your friends to kidnap somebody, would you have done it?"

"Well, no—maybe—I guess it woulda depended on how much money we was talkin' about."

"Well, Noah," Clint said, "you and your friends better find another odd job."

"Yeah, okay," Noah said, nervously.

"Now get out of here."

"Yessir!"

He ran past Clint and down the stairs. At one point, it sounded as if he fell, but then he was gone.

Clint was now sure that Lucius Randall had left town, but it wouldn't hurt to check.

***

"Can I help you, sir?" the hotel clerk asked as Clint approached the desk.

"Yes, what's your name?"

"John."

"Nice, simple. John, the young man I checked in with, who's in the room across from me," Clint said to him. "Have you seen him since last night?"

The clerk thought a moment.

"No, sir, I haven't."

"Has he checked out?"

"No, sir, he hasn't." The clerk suddenly looked concerned. "Why, isn't he in his room?"

"No," Clint said.

"I hope he hasn't run out on his hotel bill," the clerk said. "Should I be concerned. I'll have to call the sheriff and tell him—"

"Don't worry about that," Clint said. "I'll be taking care of the bill for all three rooms."

The clerk looked relieved.

***

Clint decided to go and get himself something to eat in the hotel dining room. He sat so he'd be able to keep an eye on the front door and the lobby.

During the meal, he debated with himself about whether he should wait 'til morning to tell Libbie that Lucius Randall was gone, or go up after he finished eating and tell her tonight. He decided to think about things further overnight, and see if the young man reappeared in the morning. If he didn't, and it was obvious he had left, then Clint would talk the situation over with Libbie at breakfast, and they could decide their best course of action.

***

He went back to his room after eating, spent the evening reading and keeping his ears open for the sound of Randall returning to his room. By the time he was ready to turn in, Lucius Randall still had not come back.

Clint thought he knew what it all meant, but he'd talk to Libbie about it in the morning and see if she was in agreement with him. It would probably all make much more sense when he could say it out loud.

He slept with the back of the wooden chair tucked beneath the doorknob, just for extra security.

Chapter Forty-Six

"He's what?" Libbie asked.

"Gone," Clint said. "He apparently lit out last night.

"But, why?"

"Because I caught him sneaking around," Clint said. He explained how he had followed Randall two nights before, and about the empty building. Then he told her about the man he had met, Noah Lane.

"I think Randall has been working with McMay this whole time. I think he's the one who let the Flynt family know we were in Hempstead, and I think he probably sent a telegram when he knew we were heading this way. But when I told him my theory about McMay, and that I caught him sneaking out, I think he called off whatever they had planned here—maybe another phony kidnapping—and he left town. Lane really didn't know what the job was going to be, but I'm thinking that was it."

"So where did Lucius go?"

"Probably back to Chicago," Clint said. "Once I guessed what McMay was up to, and that Randall was in cahoots with him, he didn't feel safe staying here."

"What did he think you would do to him?"

"I don't know," Clint said. "I'm angry with both him and McMay—but I'm more angry at myself."

"Why yourself?"

"Because I let myself be used," Clint said. "Let's go back to the night you and I met. Those yahoos who were heckling you at the library? I think McMay put them up to it."

"But for the love of God, why?"

"Because it would show me that you might be in some danger," Clint said. "So I let myself be used by accompanying you on the trip. And I took Randall along, believing it to be my own idea. You see? I let them use me every step of the way, and all because of my concern for you."

"I suppose I should be flattered," she said, "but now I'm angry. He financed this trip just so he could fake some kidnap attempts on me for publicity?"

"That's what I think, and with Randall running off the way he has, it's now more than just a theory."

"My God," she said, "I've been used, as well."

"Yes, but at least it was for your benefit."

"I think it was for Henry's benefit. He doesn't care about me, he just wants the books to sell."

"Either way, it works for both of you," Clint said.

"But what about the fact that the Flynt family ended up getting killed?"

"Please, don't remind me," Clint said, his heart racing. "That really makes me mad. I shot those people for no good reason."

"And I killed that woman!" Libbie said. She looked down at her breakfast plate, her appetite gone. "What are we going to do?"

"Well, since Randall's not here to escort you back to Chicago, I'm going to go with you."

"But . . . you never intended to go to Chicago."

"That's true, but now I've got some unfinished business with both Henry McMay and Lucius Randall."

"But Randall was probably only doing what McMay told him to do."

"Once we killed those three people, he could have told the truth," Clint said. "Instead, they were still planning something similar for here."

"And they were still going to go ahead with it?" she asked, incredulously. "And take the chance that somebody else might end up dead?"

"That's the way it looks."

"But . . . what will you do when we get to Chicago?"

"Well, I'm not going to kill anyone, if that's what you're thinking," Clint said, "but I'm sure I can put a scare into McMay and Lucius. The other question is, what are you going to do, Libbie?"

"Oh, I've already decided," she said. "I'm going to take the first book back from Henry, make him recall all the copies he's sent out, and then I'll find myself a new publisher—one with scruples."

"McMay will try to talk you out of it," Clint said. "He'll say he was only trying to sell books."

"He can talk until he's blue in the face," she said. "Look, you can think what you like about my husband, but George had integrity. And so do I. I won't keep myself aligned with a man like Henry McMay."

"Good for you," Clint said.

"When can we head for Chicago?" she asked.

"Right away, if you're done with your research here," he said.

"Oh, I'm finished," she said. "I'm no longer as close to starting the second book as I thought. First, I have to disentangle myself from a man who, truth be told, I never really liked in the first place. I should have listened to my instincts and kept looking for a publisher, elsewhere."

"You've got plenty of time, Libbie, to place your books elsewhere."

Chapter Forty-Seven

When Henry McMay looked up as Clint entered his office, there was no indication that he was feeling any sort of nerves. By now Lucius Randall had returned to Chicago, and had told McMay that Clint knew—or had theorized—about what they had done. Why wasn't the man showing any concern?

"Mr. Adams," McMay said, "I've been waiting for you to arrive."

"I'll bet," Clint said.

"Is Mrs. Custer with you?"

"She's in her hotel," Clint said, "I told her I wanted to talk to you first, before she did."

"Good, good," McMay said, "I have a lot to explain to her."

"To her?" Clint asked. "What about me? Don't you owe me some explanations? Maybe even an apology?"

"No, no, Mr. Adams," McMay said, "you're going to be well paid for your time—"

"That still doesn't make up for my being used," Clint said. "And then there's the fact that I killed two phony kidnappers."

"Well now, it seems to me that was their fault, and no one else's. They should have been smarter than to go for their guns against the Gunsmith, don't you think?"

"McMay," Clint said, "I should drag you out of your chair and pistol whip you."

Clint was satisfied to finally see some concern on the publisher's face.

"Now, see here—"

"No, you see here," Clint said. "You obviously have no intention of apologizing to me. What about to Libbie Custer?"

"For what? Trying to sell more copies of her book? I'm sure I can make her understand—"

"No, I don't think so," Clint said. "I'm pretty sure she's done with you, and wants her book back."

"Really?" McMay asked. "I'm afraid that would have to be something for our lawyers to discuss."

"Good luck with that," Clint said. "Just wait until the word gets out about the phony kidnapping and, oh, the glass in her sandwich on the train."

"Now, wait, wait," McMay said, looking for something on his desk. "I can prove I had nothing to do with that. I mean, why would I take a chance that she might bite into something like that?"

"And what's your proof?" Clint asked.

"It's here, somewhere . . . here it is . . . do you know someone named Victor Lazlo?"

"He was the security man on the train."

"Exactly. According to this telegram—and it was sent to you care of me, by the way—after you left the train he caught the man involved. Apparently, he had been clinging to the undercarriage of one of the train cars."

"Let me see that."

McMay handed it over. Lazlo wrote that the man had recognized Mrs. Custer at the station, and made a split second decision to get on the train and try to harm her. Apparently, his brother had been under Custer's command at the Little Bighorn.

"So you see? I had nothing to do with that."

"That may well be the case," Clint said, folding the telegram and putting it in his pocket to show Libbie, "but you can't deny you had Lucius hire the Flynt family to pull that phony kidnapping in Hempstead. And as a result, three people ended up dead."

"Not by my hand," McMay said.

"Well, there are some gentlemen waiting outside who you can explain that to," Clint said.

He went to the office door, which he had left ajar for easy listening.

"Gents?"

Two men in dark suits entered the room, and stared at McMay.

"Henry McMay, I want you to meet Federal Marshals Ethan Butterworth and Phil Carey," Clint said. "Marshals, this is the man I told you about."

"What the hell is this?" McMay said. "are these men really going to—"

They cut him off by taking out their badges and showing them to him.

"Mr. McMay, we need you to come along with us," Marshal Butterworth said.

"Is this a joke?" McMay asked.

"It's no joke, sir," Marshal Carey said. "Causing the death of three people is a serious crime."

"But . . . I didn't kill anyone," McMay said. As Clint headed for the door the Marshals went around behind McMay's desk, grabbed his arms and lifted him to his feet.

"Adams!" McMay shouted. "You can't do this!"

"And Mr. McMay," Butterworth said as Clint left, "we need to find a man named Lucius Randall . . ."

Clint left the building, heading back to the hotel to tell Libbie Custer she would probably be having no trouble disentangling herself and her books from Henry McMay's publishing company.

Coming June 27, 2019

THE GUNSMITH
448
The Fantastic Mr. Verne

**For more information
click here:** www.SpeakingVolumes.us

On Sale Now!

THE GUNSMITH *series*
Books 430 – 445

For more information
visit:

Coming Soon!

Lady Gunsmith 7
Roxy Doyle and the James Boys

**For more information
visit**: www.SpeakingVolumes.us

On Sale Now!

**Lady Gunsmith 6
Roxy Doyle and
the Desperate Housewife**

**For more information
visit:** www.SpeakingVolumes.us

On Sale Now!

Lady Gunsmith *series*
Books 1-5

**For more information
visit:** www.SpeakingVolumes.us

On Sale Now!

On Sale Now!

TRACKER *series*
by Award-Winning Author
Robert J. Randisi (J.R. Roberts)

On Sale Now!

MOUNTAIN JACK PIKE *series*
by Award-Winning Author
Robert J. Randisi (J.R. Roberts)

**For more information
visit:** www.SpeakingVolumes.us

50% Off
Audiobooks